A red-orange fireball tore through the roof of the building, spewing flames and debris. In the sky overhead, Major Sam McGee saw the city center turn red in that instant but it was too late for evasive tactics.

The fuselage shook. The bomb bay was open; the electronic jamming pod was extended as he was making his "run," a jamming run on the Iraqi air defenses to determine their accuracy. The mission, code-named *Ghost Rider*, had been designed to test the Iraqi ability to detect stealth fighters.

In that instant everything that could go wrong, went wrong . . .

On the digital tracking screen in the hangar at As Salamiyah, the stealth's signature disappeared.

Also by Tom Willard

Strike Fighters
Bold Forager
War Chariot
Sudden Fury
Red Dancer

Published by
HarperPaperbacks

STRIKE FIGHTERS

DESERT STAR

TOM WILLARD

HarperPaperbacks
A Division of HarperCollins*Publishers*

This is a work of fiction. The characters, incidents, and dialogues are products of the author's imagination and are not to be construed as real. Any resemblance to actual events or persons, living or dead, is entirely coincidental.

HarperPaperbacks *A Division of* HarperCollins*Publishers*
10 East 53rd Street, New York, N.Y. 10022

Cover art by Attila Hejja

First printing: June 1991

Printed in the United States of America

HarperPaperbacks and colophon are trademarks of HarperCollins*Publishers*

10 9 8 7 6 5 4 3 2 1

For my father-in-law and mother-in-law, Lloyd and Dorothy Lipp; my brother and sister-in-law, Steve and Trini Lipp; my brother and sister-in-law, Bruce and Val Lipp; and my brother and sister-in-law, John and Julie LeDuc.

And especially for the brave people of Kuwait, who have waited for Justice. May your wait soon be over.

Prologue

Kuwait City.
2000.

MOHAMMAD REZA MOSTAFAVI SLIPPED QUIETLY through the darkness looming over the burned-out shops and buildings along Fahed Al-Salim Street, or rather, what had once been called Fahed Al-Salim. The name had since been changed, like the Al-Sabah hospital. Everything had changed. What was most difficult was ignoring the arrogant Iraqi soldiers sitting in their armored personnel carriers and TU-72 tanks. But he did ignore them, knowing this was not the time to stare the Iraqis in the eyes; it was a gesture many Kuwaitis had paid for with their lives since the invasion.

The Iraqis didn't like the loathsome stares of the people they had annexed in the name of the Arab revolution.

Mostafavi wanted to vomit at such a thought. It was the wealth of the nation the Iraqis wanted; wealth needed to replenish the war chest that had been badly drained during the war with Iran.

Along the street were the constant reminders of the brutal Iraqi presence in the capital city.

Bullet holes marred the buildings; windows were broken. Automobile showroom floors stood empty after the pillaging invaders swooped down and stole the plush cars from their rightful owners.

Allah! They have even removed the lampposts!

The worst reminder lay on the sidewalk where Mostafavi walked. Young men, their hands and feet bound, littered the streets and alleys. The smell filled the air. Even at night the buzzing of flies was a painful reminder. The figure of a young man, his hands bound behind his back, lay dead in the gutter. Flies buzzed in his face, black now from decomposition since his murder.

Yes—murder!

Not death. Death came naturally. Murder was the name for a young man being tied and shot by cowards who were raping his land.

Where were the Americans?

That was what had swept through the underground resistance in those first few days. After several weeks, the cry became a murmur until it was no longer heard. That was when Mostafavi took action, as he was doing now in the late hours of the night.

His photographic mind was taking pictures of each Iraqi position; the number of soldiers was being recorded. He would transcribe the information later on a detailed map he was preparing.

Preparing for whom? He often wondered. Then he remembered with a heated passion: for *us*!

"Halt!" A loud, gruff voice called.

Mostafavi froze.

"Raise your hands and stand against the building." A soldier was approaching from across the street. In the dim light from the moon, he could see the soldier wore the pipings of the Iraqi paratroopers—the dogs who landed on the beach in the early hours of the attack.

"I have nothing of value." Mostafavi pleaded. It was difficult to hide the anger he felt, but he did.

"What are you hiding?" The soldier was pointing at Mostafavi's pocket. Mostafavi's left hand was thrust deep into the pocket of his coat.

"Nothing. My word to Allah."

The soldier raised his weapon. The coldness of the AK-47's barrel was nearly as cold as the look on the Iraqi's face.

"Remove your hand from the pocket. Slowly." The soldier ordered.

Mostafavi's hand came out slowly. The soldier's eyes widened momentarily in genuine surprise. And shock.

"Are you a thief?" asked the soldier.

Holding up his left arm, a shiny, steel hook protruded from an artificial arm hidden by the sleeve. Mostafavi nearly laughed. In Iraq, the hands of thieves were still severed when caught stealing, but not in Kuwait. He wanted to tell the soldier if thievery were punished by amputation, every soldier in Saddam Hussein's army would return to Iraq with both hands missing, as well as their feet.

"No. I'm not a thief. I'm an oil worker. I lost my hand in an accident."

The soldier grumped. "Take it off. It will make an interesting toy for my children."

Mostafavi felt his dignity reach the depths of tolerance.

Take my arm! Shamoot! You've taken my country, taken my nation's wealth. Now you want to take my arm!

A coldness settled over Mostafavi. "Yes. For your children. My arm will make a wonderful gift."

In the next instant the soldier's eyes widened as Mostafavi's left arm sliced upward, the open hook driving toward the soldier's throat. Two highly-sharpened, stainless steel hooks speared into the soldiers throat, straddling each side of the larynx.

A stream of dark blood pulsed as Mostafavi turned the hooks, severing the carotid artery and slicing through the vocal cords.

Holding with all his strength, Mostafavi kept the soldier at arm's length, standing upright while jerking his neck, forcing the life to flow faster from the Iraqi soldier.

In what seemed an eternity, he felt the soldier go limp, then allowed the body to pitch forward. He caught the soldier and dragged him into an alley. There, in the darkness, he tried to compose himself and think.

His mind raced. When the body was found, the Iraqis would seek revenge on his people. The resistance in the city was killing Iraqi soldiers by the scores. For each Iraqi killed, twenty Kuwaitis were executed in their place.

Then the breeze brought him the answer—the foul smell of the bodies rotting in the streets, butchered by the Iraqis and left to be feasted on at night by the rats that now swarmed through the city.

In that instance, he knew what to do. He quickly stripped off the soldier's uniform and undershorts until the man was naked. Taking the laces from the boots, he tied the soldier's hands behind his back, then bound the feet.

Noticing the blood, he whispered to the dead man. "By tomorrow morning when you're found, the rats will have eaten your face away. No one will recognize you. Not even your mother. The soldiers will think you're just another Kuwaiti killed by one of their soldiers."

He hawked, then spit on the dead man's head.

Moving silently, he went back to the street, hugging the shadows until he reached a burned-out shop on the bottom floor of a building, a building he owned. His shop.

Quietly, he slipped through the open window now void of glass and went to the rear of the shop. A walnut-panel wall was all that remained. Everything else had been removed by the Iraqis. Taking a small, plastic box from his pocket, he pressed a button.

An electric whir followed as the wall moved toward him.

Beyond the wall was a small anteroom. Another door, much larger, made of shiny steel, separated the anteroom from the heart of Mostafavi's secured walk-in vault—a vault that had more features than to merely protect the coins he sold in his shop.

Mohammad Reza Mostafavi was an arms dealer. An arsenal lay on the other side.

Reaching to the large combination dial on the door, he carefully dialed the correct combination. On the third combination, horizontal locking pins pneumatically snapped away from the locked position. Pulling on the handle, he opened the door and walked into the vault.

The coolness of the room was pleasing after the heat. He rested for a moment, then looked up. What greeted him was fear. Fear that could be tasted.

And the muzzles of four M-16 automatic rifles.

"Relax, my brothers. All is well. My apologies for being late. It could not be helped."

Standing in the hermetically sealed room, not a sound was heard except the hum of the air conditioner fed by an underground cable spliced into the city power source. Not even the Kuwaiti government knew of the cable splice, which meant the splice was also a secret from the Iraqis.

Only a few people on earth knew about Mohammad Mostafavi's secret room in back of his coin shop where he now stood, locked safely away from the Iraqi's.

At that moment, most importantly, only he knew of the four armed Kuwaiti's hiding in his secret room.

Four hard, tough Kuwaitis, not the defenseless civilians the Iraqi soldiers were beating and murdering in the streets of Kuwait City.

These four men were specially trained commandos of Kuwait's emir—commandos of the palace guard.

Stepping from the shadows, an elegant man smiled gratefully at the shopkeeper.

"Are you hurt, my brother?"

"No, Your Highness," Mostafavi replied.

Prince Sabah of the royal family asked another question. "And the Americans?"

Mostafavi smiled. "I have sent them a message. A man will come. His name is Sacrette. Boulton Sacrette. He is a fighter pilot."

"What makes you think he will come?" asked the prince.

Mostafavi smiled. "Because I have asked him Your Highness."

PART ONE: THE PLAYERS

Kurdistan. Northern Iraq.

CAPTAIN NORWOOD CULLEN DONALDSON STOOD AT the rear of a Hercules C-130, teasing the air slip thundering beneath the lowered ramp with his extended foot. Dressed in black fatigues, he wore a helmet, night vision goggles, and a freefall parachute. Behind him, seated along the hull of the massive transport, forty men in similar dress sat in the red glow of the jump light mounted at the exit door.

Gripping the anchorline cable threading through the center of the hull, he walked along the line of combat soldiers, checking each man, looking for loose straps, or weapons gurneys not properly connected to the parachute harness.

He was pleased by what he found, and smiling, his face appeared demonic in the red glow, as though he were something belched from hell.

He paused by a surly, flatfaced Scotsman putting on

gloves. The tattoo of the British Special Air Services, the SAS, was visible on his wrist.

"Who Dares—Wins!" was engraved on the skin beneath the tattoo of a sword superimposed onto airborne wings.

Donaldson knelt and motioned for six men to join him. Taking a map, he unfolded it on the deck and went over the mission a final time.

This was the night for perfection.

"Jocko," he looked at a Brit, a Cockney from London. "After my team deploys, you take command of deploying the remaining teams. Your points of exit are Kirkuk, Samarra, the floodplain south of Baghdad, and Shatt al-Arab."

Jocko shook his head. He had been concerned about the extended line of deployment since joining the mission.

"That's a bloody bit of ground to cover, captain. From one end of Iraq to the other."

Donaldson laughed throatily. "The Iraqis are keeping their radar turned off to prevent the Americans from learning their exact radar positions. And since the Iraqis don't have airborne radar, they have nothing. They won't spot the aircraft. Any ground observer will simply assume it's an Iraqi transport."

Jocko reluctantly accepted this reasoning.

Donaldson looked at the other commanders. "You know your missions. I expect you to succeed. If you fail—you're on your own. Remember, there's no government support on this operation. We're bloody well into the fire and on our own. Questions?"

There were none.

The red light flashed twice, the signal from the pilot

that the aircraft was reaching the first point of deployment—the point where Donaldson and his five men would step into the blackness above Iraq.

Making a fist, Donaldson raised his hand and was joined on the ramp by the Scot and four others. One carried a large radio pack, he seemed to move with ease under the weight.

Looking through his goggles, Donaldson saw a plateau come into view. He nodded and the five men hunkered in close to him. When the hull suddenly glowed green from the jump light, the six men fell silently off the tail.

They fell for only a few seconds, then deployed their canopies. Checking his canopy, Donaldson found the square parachute inflated. He released the slider, then gripped the toggles.

Down they floated in the pristine quiet above the plain at the eastern edge of the Zagros mountains.

To the east lay Iran. To the north lay Turkey.

One hundred feet below lay Iraq.

Donaldson saw the ground coming up and pulled down on the toggles, planing up the leading edge of the canopy, braking his descent to the point that the flared touchdown was almost imperceptible.

He wrapped up his parachute and scurried for the rocks where the others were waiting. He checked his watch. It was 0105.

"The contact will meet us in twenty-five minutes. Set up a defensive perimeter." Donaldson ordered.

The soldiers deployed a few meters apart.

At 0130, they heard the scraping of leather sandals against the hard rock. Peering through his night-vision binoculars, Donaldson made out the shape of a lone man walking toward their position.

As the man neared, Donaldson slipped forward and hid behind a pile of rocks. Passing Donaldson, the man didn't see the commando rise, but he felt the harsh grip around his neck and the sharp point of a knife at his throat.

"Who are you?" asked Donaldson.

"I am Suleiman. I was sent to take you to a safe place."

Donaldson judged him to be an old man by the sound of the voice and the thick carpet of hair on his face, but he recognized the name—the name given him in England before departure.

The six shadowy figures followed the old man to a point where a narrow trail started down from the plateau. Suleiman stopped, then whistled softly into the darkness. Another Kurd appeared, carrying a rifle.

Suleiman pointed to the younger man.

"Who the bloody hell is that?" Donaldson demanded.

Suleiman chuckled. "We keep guards posted over our village to warn us if the Iraqis come. I will relieve him. He will take you to my house. Get some rest. You can begin the rest of your journey in the morning."

Donaldson nodded. The team followed the young man down the goat trail.

When alone, Suleiman stared up at the stars, wondering if he had made the right decision.

He thought about why he had decided to assist: they had come to help destroy the Iraqis. That's what he had been told two weeks before when he made the agreement to help. The man was a stranger, but an Arab. He was polite, and knew the misery of the Kurd. He had come in the night and left in the night. His voice was like that of a man talking with gravel in his mouth. Part of his face was destroyed, no doubt by the Iraqis.

Like Suleiman, the Arab's hatred for the Iraqis could not be suppressed.

2

As Salamiyah Airbase. Saudi Arabia. 0300.

THE CRESCENT SHAPE OF THE MOON HUNG LIKE A curved sword over the Dahna Desert, a barren, ancient wasteland once forgotten except for a few archeologists and wandering bedouin tribesmen. It was dry, hot by day and cold by night. The wind never stirred on the desert except during a sirocco, a sandstorm, and then it raged, and the sand rendered to nothing everything it touched.

United States Air Force Major Sam McGee loved the desert. He had learned years before the desert was a part of nature requiring understanding, especially if one were to survive its treachery, heat, and inescapable curtain of emptiness.

McGee had first come to the desert in 1985, a desert on the opposite side of the world from As Salamiyah airbase in Tonopah, Nevada, where he had trained in the operation and testing of the best-kept secret in the United States: the FY-117A project—the stealth *Strike/Fighter!*

On a hot, sunbright day in August, the Iraqi army invaded neighboring Kuwait, setting in motion the massive military operation known as Desert Shield. McGee and his 176th Tactical Fighter Squadron were summoned from their headquarters at Edwards AFB. Loaded onto massive Galaxy C-5A transports, twenty-two stealth fighters were deployed to secret bases throughout Saudi Arabia; bases that lay beyond the range of the Iraqis Soviet-made Scud-B and Iraqi-made el-Hussein missiles.

"Good morning, Major McGee," a voice called from the hangar where McGee's stealth *Strike/Fighter* was being rolled onto the tarmac.

McGee was dressed in his flight suit, torso harness, and speed jeans; he was carrying his helmet. McGee knew he was about to embark on a mission some might think unnecessarily risky—a "ghost mission"—in essence, a mission that did not exist; a mission designed to answer questions.

Iraqi radar installations were not operating for fear the Americans could target their locations. A method was to be tested to determine if the radar could be located without being turned on. An electronic pod designed to search for radar-emitter residue had been designed by McDonnell Douglas for just this purpose.

"Good morning, Mr. Feinberg," McGee spoke to the shadow that was approaching alongside the fighter. Feinberg walked with a noticeable limp, looking like a man being pulled along while walking a large dog.

McGee knew there was a reason for the limp. Aaron Feinberg was a short, muscular man from Brooklyn.

Keen-eyed, sharp-minded, he had once served in the Israeli air force after retiring from the U.S. air force where he flew F-4s in Vietnam. After losing a leg during the Yom Kippur war, he found himself working for the Mossad, Israeli intelligence. That was before his wife died and he returned to the United States where another government agency sought his expertise—the select intelligence-gathering agency of the Joint Chiefs of Staff: the Defense Intelligence Agency.

Feinberg was a specialist on Arab aviation; specifically, Iraqi military aviation. He was now chief of security for the various stealth fighters deployed from the 176th Tactical Fighter Squadron.

Over the years Feinberg had supervised several missions in the deployment of the FY-117A, most notably, the invasion of Panama. Tonight, the mission codenamed Ghost Rider One was to be another of the many "black operations" run by the DIA.

McGee was the only black pilot in the squadron. If downed inside enemy territory, he would fit in better than the blue-eyed, blond-haired pilots of the squadron. The last thing DoD wanted was an American pilot to fall into the hands of the Iraqis.

Feinberg glanced up at the sky. "I envy you, major. It's a pilot's night for flying." His voice sounded distant.

McGee knew Feinberg ached to be back in the sky. Once a fighter pilot, always a fighter pilot.

After going ballistic on a supersonic, needle-nosed weapons platform, nothing else could ever be quite as satisfying.

"Yes, sir." McGee took a deep breath. His dark eyes roamed the sky, glanced at the moon, and finally settled on the aircraft.

"Are you ready?" asked Feinberg.

McGee's teeth flashed white. "I've been ready since my first day at the skunk works."

Feinberg chuckled. The Skunk Works—the super-secret Lockheed facility where the stealth FY-117A was built, as well as the SR-71 Blackbird spy plane and the U-2's.

Feinberg pointed at the stealth fighter. "We'll have the package ready in short order."

McGee looked at the stealth. The bomb bay doors were open; extending from the aircraft was a weapons pylon. Three men were carrying a black cylindrical pod to the pylon.

McGee stepped over to the wing-shaped fighter. Running his hand along the leading edge of the RAM, the radar absorbent material surface, he said, "I'd prefer a couple of Mavericks."

The FY-117A normally carried two AGM-65D Maverick air-to-ground guided missiles. Tonight, there would be none, only the electronics pod.

"Next time, McGee," Feinberg replied.

McGee nodded disappointedly. "Yes, sir. Next time."

Feinberg took out a map and spread the flight chart on the ground. Both men knelt.

Feinberg looked at McGee. "Let's quickly go over the mission. After take-off, you'll fly to coordinates FS82. You'll take on fuel from an air force KC-135 near the Saudi-Iraqi border, then make your run. After completing your mission, you'll refuel on the return flight at coordinates JZ23. Two navy KA-6 Intruders from the U.S.S. *Enterprise* will meet you. There will be a squadron of F-18s waiting as well in case you have anything on your tail."

McGee nodded. "Tell them not to be late."

Feinberg extended his hand. The young and old held the grip for a long moment.

"I'll tell them," Feinberg said softly.

McGee nodded sharply. "Let's get it on."

The pilot climbed into the cockpit, slipped on his helmet, connected his torso harness to the parachute lugs on the ejection seat, then began the start-up.

Slowly, the stealth fighter rolled onto the runway. A loud, ear-aching whine followed as the power build-up began. Increasing the power to full throttles, the fighter did not leave a bright firetail burning in its wake as other fighter aircraft did. The FY-117A did not have after-burner capability, that would be counterproductive to the purpose of stealth. Instead, the twin General Electric F404-GE-100A turbofans 34,000 pounds of thrust were neatly directed through low heat-signature reducing slots in the trailing edge of the fuselage.

The fighter didn't shoot straight up in a vertical climb; rather, the black machine stayed low, hugging the ground effect above the Dahna Desert. Reaching maximum air-speed of mach 0.8, McGee set in his course on the inertial navigation system, establishing waypoint coordinates to intercept the KC-135.

Activating the computer, he felt the controls come under the command of the fly-by-wire computer system.

Behind his faceplate, his mouth suddenly widened into a grin, and he whispered softly to the computer, using the pet name he had given it.

"Giles, take me to Baghdad!"

3

Baghdad, Iraq.
0440.

COLONEL ABU AZ AHMEDSA WAS TALL AND THIN, with a toothbrush moustache and wide, dancing eyes. Almost comical in appearance, he often recalled being at an American embassy party where he was told by the CHUSMLO, chief United States military liaison officer, that he looked like a tall version of an Arabic Charlie Chaplin. Ahmedsa thought that funny; he was a fan of Charlie Chaplin. He was even a fan of the Americans, though they now stood perched for war on the borders of his country, a war Ahmedsa did not want to see happen.

He was driving along Rashid Street, toward the center of the capital, negotiating the gauntlet of roadblocks established by the army, which was running the tightest security checks Ahmedsa could remember, even tighter than during the war with Iran.

Checking his watch, he eased his BMW to a stop in front of a roadblock where three soldiers approached brandishing AK-47 assault rifles.

The first soldier, a sergeant, smiled admiringly at the BMW, knowing it was fresh from the showrooms of Kuwait City—a "repatriated revolutionary vehicle" brought to Baghdad by the Iraqi army.

Recognizing the rank on Ahmedsa's shoulder boards, the sergeant saluted. "*Salom allakhim.*"

Ahmedsa returned the salute and handed his papers to the sergeant. Carefully, as though looking disinterested, he slowly scanned the defensive positions twenty meters off the boulevard.

Looming from behind a necklace of sandbags, a Soviet 2S1 SO-122 Gvozdika self-propelled, medium-artillery, armored vehicle sat beneath camouflaged netting, its massive 122mm howitzer gun extending from the turret. One of the crew sat stradling the gun; intermittently, the glow of a cigarette burned from above the gun.

Thirty meters from the Gvozdika, a Uragan BM-27 rocket launcher vehicle was nestled within similar sandbags and camouflaging. Soft music drifted into the night from behind the sandbags.

Ahmedsa made a mental notation of the emplacement, recalling how the two emplacements were not there yesterday afternoon when he returned home from the secret command bunker in the center of the city.

"Have a prosperous morning, colonel." The sergeant was grinning, his teeth brown from tea stains. Ahmedsa took the papers and nodded, then pressed the accelerator to the floor.

Fifteen minutes and two security checks later, Ahmedsa reached the center of the city. The Ishtar Sheraton, once an elegant hotel, now stood in blackness, as did the rest of city during the crisis; surrounding the hotel were more gun emplacements, more soldiers, and a battery of air-to-air mobile missile launchers.

The hotel was one of many secured locations spread around the city; the president of Iraq was a cautious man. Treachery was an art he understood, an art in which he was an expert; by constantly moving he would be able to avoid assassination.

Or so he thought, mused Ahmedsa, hauling his heavy briefcase from the BMW and marching briskly toward the entrance to the Sheraton. He hurried past the security checkpoints to the elevator on the main floor.

Stepping into the elevator, Ahmedsa started to press the fourteenth floor button when another officer suddenly hurried into the car.

Ahmedsa stiffened. Lieutenant Fazi Moskuk smiled politely, but kept his eyes straight ahead. One of Hussein's favorites, the loyal young officer was one of the president's aides.

"Why are you here this early, Lieutenant Moskuk?" asked Ahmedsa. "I would think the president's aides would be home sleeping."

Moskuk nodded politely, then tapped a briefcase he was carrying. "This arrived thirty minutes ago." He looked around, as though the walls of the elevator might have eyes and ears. "Our agents inside Saudi Arabia have plotted all the American military installations."

Ahmedsa nodded understandably. The information would be invaluable.

A thought suddenly came into Ahmedsa's mind. "I have important intelligence information for the president; he is expecting my arrival. It is late. We are both tired and should be home in bed with our women. Perhaps I can give the president your data when I present him the other intelligence data. You can go home and be with your lovely new bride."

Moskuk thought about the proposition for a long, careful moment. Finally, he shook his head. "No, colonel. I appreciate your concern, but I better deliver the tape. You *know* how the president can be."

Yes, thought Ahmedsa. *I know how the Butcher of Baghdad can be.*

"As you wish," replied Ahmedsa, who leaned ever so slightly into the corner of the elevator.

When he turned and faced Moskuk, his right hand went to the control panel where his fingers pressed the stop button.

Moskuk looked alarmed as the elevator suddenly halted, then his eyes widened as he saw Ahmedsa's left hand.

Allah!

Moskuk lunged at Ahmedsa, but the intelligence officer was prepared for the attack. As the young officer's body slammed forward, Ahmedsa's left hand came up at a thirty-degree angle. In the soft glow of the elevator light, Moskuk saw the blade gleam only for a moment.

A hot, searing shaft of pain followed, starting beneath Moskuk's sternum, then racing up his torso into his throat, where the scream he was aching to release was trapped by Ahmedsa's powerful hand clamping his mouth.

Moskuk's eyes bulged; his knees buckled, but his weight was held off the floor by the intelligence officer's knee, driven into Moskuk's crotch.

Ahmedsa held the dying man; he felt the life race from

his body, felt his heartbeat grow weaker as the pulse played along the blade into Ahmedsa's clenched hand.

When Ahmedsa heard the young officer's sphincter release, and smelled the foul waste of death, he pulled the knife out and lowered the body to a sitting position beneath the control panel.

Moving quickly, he reached into his breast pocket and removed a pack of cigarettes. Tearing off the cellophane seal, he dumped the contents into the palm of his hand.

A black detonator lay framed within his extended fingers. Quickly, Ahmedsa removed the backing and opened the briefcase. Inside, thirty pounds of Czech Symtex lay in neat blocks. Attaching the transmitter to a wire running from one block, Ahmedsa pressed the timer on the detonator.

Next, he checked his watch. Four minutes. From another pocket he removed a single cigarette and lit the Galoise, his favorite. Smoke drifted through the enclosed elevator as he glanced at Moskuk.

He checked his watch. Two minutes.

It was time!

Reaching to the control panel, he pressed another button, freeing the elevator car. The downward movement reminded him that time was critical.

When the door opened, he shielded Moskuk's body from the guard in the lobby and reached inside and pressed the button marked fourteen. The doors closed and he waited for the hum as the elevator started up to where President Saddam Hussein was being briefed by other officers in Ahmedsa's intelligence unit.

Ahmedsa started for the door. A guard, watching him suddenly rose to his feet. His hand shot out. He was pointing at Ahmedsa!

Ahmedsa looked at his shirt. Horror suddenly shot across his features.

Blood! His victim's crimson-red blood.

Ahmedsa dashed for the main entrance. Shouts pursued him as the intelligence officer went for the leather holster on his hip.

Slamming through the entrance, pistol gripped in his hand, Ahmedsa suddenly heard a roar that swept from behind, lifting him and carrying him forward on a wave of nausea and pain.

He didn't have to look at his shirt. He felt the impact of the bullets as they struck his back and burst through his rib cage, splintering bone, shredding lung, taking his life.

Pitching forward, Ahmedsa bounced off a sandbag wall, then fell forward, his eyes turned to the crescent blade of the moon.

That was when he heard another roar. Then, against the white of the crescent moon he saw a silhouette.

Small, moving with the speed of lightning, a wing-shaped outline was there for just a single moment.

The explosion that followed was not from the fighter, but from the high explosives in the elevator.

A red-orange fireball tore through the roof of the building, spewing flames and debris into the sky.

On the street in front of the Sheraton, Ahmedsa was smothered by tons of concrete. He died believing he had succeeded.

In the sky overhead, Major Sam McGee saw the city center turn red in that instant but it was too late for evasive tactics.

The fuselage shook. The bomb bay was open; the

electronic jamming pod was extended as he was making his run, a jamming run on the Iraqi air defenses to determine their accuracy.

Everything that could go wrong, was going wrong.

4

0515.

"GODDAMN!" FEINBERG BREATHED HEAVILY. HE WAS staring at a digital tracking screen in the hangar at As Salamiyah. An E-3 AWACS was on station over Saudi Arabia transmitting the stealth's location with a link-up from the KH-12 recon-navsat.

The stealth's signature had disappeared.

Feinberg smoothed his face roughly, then gulped the remnants of coffee from a styrofoam cup. Looking around, he could see the faces of the technicians turned in his direction.

Failure. And Feinberg knew in whose court the ball was now bouncing. After walking in circles for a few minutes, Feinberg went to the red telephone sitting beside the tracking screen. He didn't need to dial a number. The line was a direct link-up to the Joint Chiefs in the Pentagon.

In a soft voice, Feinberg said, "Let me speak to the

chairman." Moments later, the voice of the Chairman of the Joint Chiefs was on the other end.

Asked for a situation report, Feinberg replied, "We've lost *Ghost Rider One!*"

0555.

Suleiman Ratab was an old man whose ancient eyes had seen too much. His body was wracked by the corrosion of age; his brain filled with the agony of remembrance. Remembrance—that gnawing disease God had given all men to carry with them forever. What he hated was that there was no good remembrance; only bad. Why? He often asked himself. Why could he not have pleasurable remembrances?

There was no answer. Only the biting pain of remembrance. First, the Ottoman Turks of his childhood in Kurdistan. Then, as a young man he was ruled by the Hasemites. Finally, the Iraqis.

The Iraqis were not the most brutal, yet they were the most fiendish.

"*Allah!* What have we done to deserve this punishment!" He shouted to the graying morning from the cliff overlooking his village near the Tigris.

There was no answer. Just the remembrance of the foul-tasting yellow gas that swept through his village on the wind they called Satan's Breath.

The gas. Nerve. Killing. Twisting the faces of the beautiful children into grotesque masks worse than he ever saw while once watching the fanatical self-inflicted torture of the Whirling Dervishes.

Wearing a goatskin coat and sandals, an old Enfield rifle slung to his shoulder, Suleiman sat back down on the loam-colored rocks of his guard post and squinted his eyes as the sun crawled lazily to the horizon.

Raising a leather flask above his head, he squeezed until a stream of arak flowed into his mouth. Arak was forbidden by the Koran; since it was home brewed, it was the only distilled spirit available to the Kurds.

Staring at the flask, he felt a momentary wave of shame; then the arak took effect and the pain was soothed, the shame lessened. God had spared him. God had given him life when the children were dying around him the day the Iraqis bombed the village. God would not punish him for drinking the arak. He had been punished enough.

Now he stood guard, along with others, watching the sky and the road winding through the mountain. Watching—for they might come again.

Certainly, God was now being gracious. Had he not sent the Butcher of Baghdad off to Kuwait in search of new spoils? Perhaps the Kurds would be left alone.

Perhaps. . . .

That was when the sky shook and Suleiman felt the ground tremble. Looking up, he turned quickly to the west. From the shadows beneath the mountains a dark image appeared. A bird? Perhaps a vulture, there were many in the rocky desert.

A low, piercing whine bored through his brain; his ears ached and he thought his heart would explode as the black shape suddenly veered off, as if the hand of God had turned the creature from the path aimed directly at Suleiman.

Like lightning, the image was there—then gone—swooping behind a tall promontory of rock.

Suleiman's old legs pulled his weight upward, then pushed him along the craggy ground. Ahead stood the promontory. He raced with all his strength toward what seemed to be the screams of a thousand demons echoing through the early morning air; sounds of rocks breaking, metal shrieking.

Then silence.

The promontory towered above a flat plateau carved onto the top of the mountain range overlooking the valley. The erosive wind had, in thousands of years, turned what was once a mountain peak into a flat plateau, leaving deep crags and grooves that wound along the surface like the tracks of large, desert snakes.

Rounding the promontory, he stood in the shadows of the tall rock formation, watching the place where the dark intruder had landed. Smoke billowed from the earth, masking the outline of whatever had landed on the plateau.

He watched for several long minutes, not moving, barely breathing, allowing the pace of his heart to settle. The machine made many noises: sparks shot out from the rear; there was a whirring sound he did not recognize.

Finally, he began walking forward; half crouched, his rifle extended, he neared the cloud of smoke.

Suddenly he stopped. The barrel of the rifle rose to greet the thinly-shadowed figure approaching through the smoke.

The Iraqis. He swore aloud.

The moment the sights were on the heart of the man, Suleiman started to squeeze the trigger. That was the moment the sun broke clear, flashing off something multicolored on the shoulder of the intruder.

A flag. A flag he recognized.

"Don't shoot!" called the voice. A man's voice, nearly muffled as he spoke while removing a strange helmet covering his entire head.

"Don't shoot, *fendi*."

Fendi. Friend.

Suleiman Ratab inched closer, his rifle never wavering, aimed at the heart.

Not ten feet from the man, the stranger suddenly fell forward, gripping his shoulder. He writhed for a moment, then lay still.

Suleiman knelt by the fallen stranger. Carefully, he ran his hand along the man's body. A spasm followed when he touched the shoulder of the stranger.

A low, pitiful moan escaped from the unconscious man's mouth.

Suleiman lay down the rifle, then took his flask and lifted the stranger's head. A stream of arak flowed onto the lips, then forehead.

Moments later the stranger's eyes opened. Dark eyes set within dark skin. Black skin.

"My name. . . ." The voice said, then faded. Momentarily, he continued. "My name is Major Sam McGee. I am an American."

McGee looked past the Kurd. Following the line of

McGee's sight, Suleiman saw the man was looking at the black shape now clearly visible where moments before the stealth fighter sat wrapped in a cocoon of billowing smoke.

When McGee reached to his pocket, Suleiman slapped the black man's hand.

McGee winced, then held up his hand indicating there was nothing to fear. He pointed at the zippered pocket on his flight suit. Suleiman unzipped the pocket and removed a small packet.

McGee said nothing. He watched breathlessly while Suleiman examined the strange device. Not realizing what he was doing, Suleiman's twisted fingers pressed a white button on the top of the communicator.

There was a beep. Suleiman dropped the transmitter.

"*Aaa-ggg-hhh!*" Suleiman's foot rose in the air, it's arc followed by the eyes of McGee, who started to yell, but was silenced by the falling foot.

Again and again Suleiman stomped the plastic shell until there was nothing left but twisted, broken circuit boards and wires of many colors.

Turning to the American, Suleiman couldn't understand the look on the pilot's face: McGee's lips were parted.

He was smiling. He knew before the transmitter had been smashed his position had been signaled to the KH-12 reconsat roaming above the Persian Gulf. From two hundred miles up, the 'KeyHole' reconaissance satellite would record his exact position.

Then the pilot of *Ghost Rider One* fell into unconsciousness.

0730.

Lt. J. G. Ryan "Rhino" Michaels, a graduate of the U.S. Naval Academy at Annapolis, learned the importance of chain of command early in his military education. Chain of command worked like a pyramid—from the point, which was the commander in chief, down through the many broadening levels of the pyramid. He figured he was somewhere near the base of the pyramid, not quite the bottom, but damn close. Close enough to the bottom so he couldn't really figure out the reasoning of the orders passed down from the top.

Then again, he wasn't paid to reason. He was paid to fly fighter planes, which meant he was close enough to the bottom so that he merely carried out the orders, whether he liked them or not.

The president of the United States had apparently given an order to the Secretary of Defense, who sits right beneath the point of the pyramid. It was probably a simple order, nothing complicated; the president didn't have much time for complication, what with budgets, Supreme Court appointments, environmental destruction, and the economy. The president probably said, "Send troops to the Persian Gulf."

This was following the 2 August 1990 invasion—or "annexation"—of Kuwait by the military juggernaut of Iraq.

Rhino called it something else. The fighter pilot from Grand Forks, North Dakota called it "the day all hell broke loose in the world."

Hell sponsored by a madman named Saddam Hussein.

The Secretary of Defense then contacted the chairman of the Joint Chiefs of Staff. That was the spot in the pyramid, three levels down from the top, where the vagueness of the president's order began to clarify through military genius.

Which meant the situation began to get complicated. Including the naming of the military effort put forth by the United States and a group of foreign countries who were fellow members of the United Nations.

The clarification began with the code-naming of the effort: Desert Shield.

By the time the trickle-down effect of the vague order had become graphically clear, hundreds of thousands of U.S. marines, paratroopers, airmen and women, ships, nuclear aircraft carriers, and warplanes were perched on Mr. Hussein's doorsteps—all of his doorsteps—from inland Saudi Arabia, to the Persian Gulf, Suez Canal, and the Mediterranean.

To Rhino, the Mediterranean was the absolute basement of the pyramid, a point he had been considering for the last hour since launching from the deck of the

U.S.S. *Valiant*, the core of the battle group code-named Zulu Station.

"This is bullshit, Gooze, pure, unadulterated, ballistic bull excrement of the highest quality. We're a rapid deployment battle group, not a border guard. We're so far from the fucking action, it'll be two days before anyone tells us if the shooting has started," Rhino snapped into the mouthpiece of his helmet. He was talking to his dashman, or wingman, flying off his starboard wing at fifteen thousand feet, what pilots call angels fifteen.

The reply from his wingman was forthcoming, though more philosophical.

"Like the CAG always says, Rhino, nobody said it would be easy being great." Lt. j. g. Sean "Gooze" Thomas replied, while glancing at Rhino. He flashed a thumbs-up, then looked off to the north.

He couldn't help thinking how on-target Rhino was. Their Strike/Fighters could have played hell on the armor columns moving down the Baghdad highway, Iraqi fighters were inept at best. So what did they have now? Border patrol off the Syrian coast. Christ! The most boring duty imaginable. They had launched two hours ago, reached angels fifteen, and then the excitement ended.

Looking out the cockpit of his fighter, he saw Cyprus, a rocky island in the center of the turquoise Mediterranean. To the south was Lebanon. The shore was white where the sea ended against the war-torn city. Smoke could be seen billowing into the upper atmosphere.

"Looks like the Lebanese are kicking each others' asses again, Rhino." He pointed to the smoke. He knew that meant artillery was raining down on the city. He couldn't help but wonder if the smoke was from Muslim, or Christian guns.

"Crazy bastards are getting an early start," said Rhino.

"Yeah," Gooze replied sarcastically. "I guess they figure by starting early they won't wake up the children."

That was when a thought came to Rhino. "Say, Gooze? Why don't we divert a few degrees, roll in, and lose some of this thunder we're carrying on our bomb racks. It'll beat the hell out of this scow duty."

"That's a thought, but one you should keep to yourself, old buddy. We're on patrol, but it's not combat patrol. Besides, we wouldn't know who to bomb in that shithole."

"Just a suggestion. Christ! I'm getting a hard-on for some action."

That was when a voice broke into the conversation, a voice the pilots would recognize in a thunderstorm.

"Knock it off, you two. This is a patrol—despite your personal observations. You're not in the sitting room of a whorehouse!"

The voice of Captain Boulton Sacrette had more bark than bite. Both younger pilots knew he was more chagrined by the carrier's deployment than anyone else in the battle group.

"Patrol for what?" Rhino shot back. He was looking now to the port, where an F/A-18 Hornet Strike/Fighter had drifted onto his nine o'clock position.

The number on the Hornet was zero-zero, the designation of the CAG, the commander of the air wing. The plane was otherwise known as Double Nuts.

"We've just received new orders from the old man."

"What new orders? Bomb Iraq?" asked Rhino.

"You wish," Sacrette replied as he repeated verbatim the amended orders from the battle group commander. "The United Nations has approved an air embargo against any and all aircraft entering Iraqi airspace."

"Another vague order from the top, right, Thunderbolt?" asked Gooze, calling Sacrette by his running name, or call-sign.

"Not exactly. This order has a few specifics: the United Nations has so resolved, by air embargo, that all Iraqi airspace is now officially off limits to all aviation except for humanitarian purposes."

"What constitutes 'humanitarian?' " Rhino asked facetiously.

Sacrette laughed. He wasn't certain either, but he knew one thing: "Any aircraft flying humanitarian supplies to Iraq is required to file a flight plan and land for inspection at the nearest friendly airport prior to entering the embargoed airspace."

"What do we do if we see an airplane flying toward Iraqi airspace?" Gooze shot back. He was looking south. Beyond the coast lay Syria, beyond Syria was Iraq. From angels fifteen he could see where the Euphrates river threaded through Iraq into Syria, then on to Turkey.

"We make radio contact and determine the aircraft's intentions. If they are flying humanitarian aid to Iraq we can verify through local channels. If they haven't been cleared, we divert the aircraft to the nearest friendly airport."

That left an opening for the obvious question:

"What if the aircraft doesn't respond to the diversion?" asked Gooze.

Sacrette laughed. "Friendly persuasion, young man, friendly persuasion."

"Hell," said Rhino. "I'd rather shoot the bastards down"

"We're not to use any firepower. Do you understand,

gentlemen? No firepower whatever. If we can't bluff them, we let them slide. Is that clear?" came back the CAG.

"Let them slide? If that's the case, why bother?" Rhino asked incredulously.

"Those are the rules of engagement." Sacrette's voice sounded with a mix of "follow your orders" and "I heard that."

Before they could respond, Sacrette's radar was projecting a blip on the heads-up display.

"We've got traffic."

The sky above the Med shook as the three F/A-18 Hornets went to full afterburner thrust. With jet fuel pumping directly into the engine exhaust flames, the fighters were riding on a carpet of fire.

Minutes later, Sacrette spotted the aircraft. Flying low to avoid radar detection, a Hercules C-130 was nearing the coast of Syria, northeast of the Lebanese border.

Sacrette changed frequencies on the HOTAS, the hands-on-throttle-and-stick. This unique feature of the Hornet allowed the pilot to operate all the systems of the fighter without removing his hands from either throttles or control stick. This included the communications and weapons systems.

"Al Ladhiqyah control, this is Red Wolf one, from the U.S.S. *Valiant*, with two aircraft, approaching Syrian airspace in pursuit of unidentified aircraft nearing your airspace. Request permission to enter Syrian airspace in pursuit."

The air base at Al Ladhiqyah sits on the Syrian coast near the Turkish border. Known for its tourism and sport fishing, it serves as Syria's coastal defense, deploying fighter aircraft and SAM missiles. As a member of the multi-national force opposing Iraq, the United States and Syria were working together for the first time in history.

After a strained pause, the voice of the control officer replied, "Permission granted. The aircraft has not requested landing clearance for inspection. Two of our fighters have been dispatched to join you. Take no action. Repeat. Take no action."

Sacrette closed onto the aircraft.

"We've got a C-130, gentlemen." He was looking below, where the massive outline of the C-130 left the blue of the Med, and became absorbed by the loam color of the Syrian countryside.

Turning on the television camera, it was mere seconds before Sacrette had the aircraft on the screen on his instrument panel.

"Type C-130 confirmed." Sacrette looked for markings. "No international markings. I'll wager Rhino's virginity this is dirty."

Rhino started to reply, but a quick glance toward Syria changed his mind. "We've got company."

Sacrette looked over at Rhino. The young pilot was pointing below. Then his voice went up a couple of octaves. "Christ, Thunderbolt. They're Flankers."

Sacrette released the tension-reel on his ejection harness and leaned as far to the right as possible. The outline of the two SU-27 Flankers was vaguely familiar, then he realized why. "They look like Hornets!" said Sacrette.

Gooze laughed. "The Russkies must have stolen our plans from McD," he said, referring to McDonnell Douglas, the designer and builder of the F/A-18.

"Knock off the chatter. Let's IFF these characters and have a talk about tactics." Sacrette punched in the identification-friend-foe frequency. The Flankers responded with the code, telling Sacrette they were part of the U.N. force.

What he wasn't prepared for was the voice that came over the radio from one of the pilots.

"This is Major Sergei Zuberov. I am requesting to speak with the leader of the American fighters."

A chill raced through Sacrette. It was over these same skies years before he had first heard Zuberov's voice, a voice that taunted a young, American, naval pilot as his aircraft twisted and fell, disintegrating toward the Bekaa Valley outside Beirut.

Zuberov and other Soviet and East German pilots were the mainstay of the Syrian air force, on loan from Moscow.

Sacrette took a deep breath. "This is Captain Boulton Sacrette, United States Navy. Good morning, major."

There was a short pause from the Russian. "Good morning, Captain Sacrette. We are joined together once again."

"It's your call, Sergei. How do you want to make the play?" asked Sacrette.

"Instruct your pilots to stand off. We will intercept and divert to your position. You can instruct them to go to Adana. That is the sector inspection airport, the American air base."

"Roger. You heard that, stand off. Fly a tight three-sixty. Give them room."

After checking in with the CAG, the three fighters began flying a tight circle.

Meanwhile the MiGs closed on the Hercules, one on each side of the nose section.

Suddenly, the Hercules swung nose up, then banked

hard right. The massive wingtip nearly struck the starboard MiG.

"What the hell is going on?" Rhino asked.

That was when Sacrette saw the port rear door of the C-130 open. Zooming the television screen, Sacrette saw a black-clad figure standing in the door. A long, cylindrical tube was raised to his shoulder.

Sacrette didn't have to guess. "Watch yourself, Sergei. There's a bandit in the port door. I believe he's carrying a Stinger missile."

The two MiGs dropped off. The man in the door leaned back. Moments later, the rear ramp lowered. Five men stood on the ramp. Each was holding a Stinger.

In the next instant, the wing beneath one of the Flankers lit up with white smoke.

"Christ! One of the MiGs has launched!"

SACRETTE SAT WATCHING THE WHITE TRAIL OF WHAT he suspected was a Soviet AA-8 Aphid, air-to-air IR heat-seeking missile, track the engine signature of the C-130.

"Those bastards in the 130 must be crazy, Thunderbolt," said Gooze. There was disgust and anticipation in his voice, like a child watching something he knew was wrong, yet found exciting.

Sacrette switched off the television camera. He wasn't certain why he made that decision. All he knew was that he didn't want anyone to see the event.

The Aphid struck the C-130 on the starboard outboard engine. A red-orange ball of flame erupted, and Sacrette could see the wing separate from the fuselage.

The C-130 began a sickening, side-to-side flop, then flattened into a spiral.

"Those poor bastards," said Rhino.

"Poor bastards, my ass. They were about to launch an

attack. The Russian responded properly," replied Sacrette, who was lowering his nose.

A thick, black plume marked the C-130's line of fall toward the Syrian desert.

Impact was followed by another explosion. Rolling out, Sacrette increased power and aimed the nose of his Hornet for the two silhouettes in the blue sky above.

"Zuberov! You were a little hasty on the trigger. You might have gotten our asses into the royal sling."

Moments later, the unsettled voice of the Soviet ace came back. "My wingman, Captain Sacrette. He fired the missile. It was not I."

"Your wingman! You're both responsible. We're all responsible. That aircraft was not a military aircraft."

Zuberov's voice was now settled. "Nonetheless, the aircraft was displaying hostile intentions. Authorization came from a higher authority than mine, captain."

"Higher authority? What higher authority?" Sacrette was now alongside the Soviet pilot. He was turned facing the Russian, his visor pulled up onto his helmet. Sacrette's cerulean eyes were burning at the Soviet pilot.

Zuberov's hand came up. "I can say nothing more, except what I have told you. Remember, this is Syria, my friend."

My friend!

The same words used by Zuberov following Operation War Chariot, the joint U.S.-Soviet air assault against the Iraqi ICBM missile complex at Al-Nasra.

My friend!

The two pilots, both sworn to kill the other, had buried the hatchet after Sacrette helped rescue Zuberov's father, a Soviet air marshal, from a group of Iranian religious fanatics holding the general for ransom.

Sacrette spoke into the mouthpiece. "There will be hell to pay, Sergei."

Zuberov appeared to shrug. "Perhaps now the game will begin with seriousness."

Looking at the Russian, he saw the Soviet raise his hand and salute.

Sacrette understood. Hundreds of thousands of troops had been ushered in to fight a war that was nothing more than a stand-off. He had sat on his hands for weeks, angered that the *Valiant* had been sent to the most remote area of the theater away from the action area. Away from where the fight would be joined—if there was a fight—and he felt certain there would be.

Sacrette returned the salute, then ordered his two fighters, "Let's take it home to the Bird Farm."

The first shot in Desert Shield had been fired!

8

ADMIRAL ELROD LORD WAS STANDING AT THE BRIDGE watching the recovery operations for the three F/A-18s led by Captain Sacrette. As commander of Battle Group Zulu station, Lord was responsible for the lives of the 6,500 men aboard the nuclear carrier U.S.S. *Valiant* and approximately 8,000 men aboard the remaining ships of the BG. Like any commander, he was responsible for the incident that took place less than a half-hour before over Syrian airspace.

Time was now of the essence. A report would have to be filed to the JCs, who in turn would report to the president. Who the president reported to was not Lord's worry. What worried him was he hadn't thought about retirement. Perhaps, now, he should give serious thought to what might be his only option.

He was angered by that thought. He had watched the "real time" televised account from Sacrette's television camera to the CIC. Those men were armed with weapons. Granted, the fighters could have layed back, made contact, tried to defuse the situation. Instead, they acted like fighter pilots: they got off the first shot, which was usually the definitive difference in a game in which there was no reward for finishing second.

The first shot!

Christ. Was it all going to start? No matter the reason, Saddam Hussein could use this incident to start the war no one wanted.

The Persian Gulf was on the brink of total war. For the first time since World War II, American forces could be exposed to rocket and aerial assault from an enemy, an enemy not afraid to use women and children as hostages to protect their military installations. An enemy not afraid to use chemical warfare on *their* enemy, or *on their own people!*

Thoughts such as these were also going through his mind, but preparations had been made for such occurrences. Daily drills in chemical responses were conducted aboard each vessel. The men knew what to do, of that he was certain. Only the unexpected would cause the greatest threat.

The unexpected—such as what had happened with the C-130.

Lord walked back to the combat information center behind the bridge. The walls were lined with radar scopes, computers, and communications systems, and manned by sailors and officers whose duty it was to fight a war from the CIC, the nerve center of the carrier. Sitting in the wash of red light illuminating the CIC, Captain Jerome Opsta, the new exec, was watching the computer beaming the location of the transmitter signal provided by Keyhole KH-12.

"We've got something unusual from KH-12, admiral." Opsta was pointing at the identification code scrawled on one of the screens.

Lord leaned into the screen and examined the code; he wasn't sure what it meant. He was, however, sure of one thing: the location from where the code was transmitting.

"Are you certain of these coordinates, captain?" asked Lord.

"Beats the hell out of me, but yes, sir, the locale's authentic."

Lord touched the screen. "Christ. It's coming from inside Iraq."

Opsta looked concerned. "Yes, sir. And if it's transmitting to KH-12, it must be one of our transmitters."

Lord looked quizzically at Opsta. "Aircraft locator beacon?"

Opsta shook his head. "No, sir. The frequency is too low. Besides, the signature is different from emergency landing transmitters."

Lord released a long sigh. Before he could say anything, Sacrette's voice came over the radio. "Thunderbolt, calling the ball. Hornet ball. Two-point-three."

Sacrette had indicated he was observing the glide slope approach provided by the fresnel lense, a landing light system used for landing approach aboard a carrier. Hornet was the aircraft type to set the ball at the proper approach setting for the F/A-18. Two-point-three meant remaining fuel in thousands of pounds—2,300 pounds.

Lord went to the bridge. In the distance he could see Sacrette's aircraft approaching the rear landing area of the carrier.

He thought about the CAG, and their long relationship which may soon be terminated.

Sacrette was a tall, wiry Montanan of French-Canadian descent. He was responsible for the more than 100 aircraft deployed on the carrier and other ships in the BG. He, too, took his job seriously.

A former F-14 Tomcat pilot, he had trained Iranian pilots during the Shah of Iran's regime, pilots trained to fight the Iraqis.

Sacrette had fought the Iraqis as early as the past year during Operation War Chariot.

The two men had known each other since Sacrette had graduated from flight school during the Vietnam War and roared onto the deck of the *Kitty Hawk* where Lord had been the CAG. He often recalled that day, remembering the shocking sight that greeted him as Sacrette opened the cockpit of his F-4 Phantom.

"What is that creature, lieutenant?" Lord asked incredulously.

"My RIO. His name is Martini. He's a fair hand, except when he takes a leak on my shoulder."

Sitting on Sacrette's shoulder was a chimpanzee. Martini became the mascot of the squadron and Sacrette went on to become one of a handful of aces in the southeast Asian war.

Martini was lost over the Red River Valley of North Vietnam when his F-4 was destroyed by a SAM missile.

Sacrette survived and stayed in the navy. He was from cattle country, but wanted to lead men in combat, not cattle over a cattle guard.

Lord now recalled what Sacrette said following the raid against Al-Nasra: "We should have finished off the entire military."

Releasing a long sigh of frustration, Lord said wearily, "You might get your chance, captain. You might get your chance."

Sacrette's Hornet landed on the deck, grabbed wire three, then the air roared as the CAG shoved the throttles to full afterburner. This was to insure that if the grappling cable didn't hold the aircraft, the Hornet would have power for a take-off roll, thus insuring the plane didn't roll over the bow of the ship.

In the background gooze's voice could be heard over the radio as he approached the "trap," the arresting cables on the deck of the *Valiant,* at over 140 mph.

"Red Wolf four. Hornet ball. Three-point-two."

Moments later, the aircraft slammed onto the deck. Within minutes, the three fighters were recovered and on the elevators, being lowered to the hangar deck.

Lord went to the telephone. "This is the admiral. I want Captain Sacrette and Lieutenants Michaels and Thomas to report to the bridge. Immediately!"

9

"WHAT IN THE SAM-HELL DID YOU THINK YOU WERE doing, captain?" Lord yelled in Sacrette's face. He was nearly apoplectic. "You have just committed a violation that will, no doubt, earn you—hell—all of us, a very long stay in the Portsmouth Naval prison! *If* we're not shot by a firing squad."

"They only use firing squads during wartime, sir," said Thomas.

Lord's eyeballs were popping. "Precisely, young lieutenant. You may have just started a goddamned war."

"We didn't fire the missile, sir. The Syrian flying as Major Zuberov's wingman fired on the Herky, and I believe they had just cause. There were men armed with Stingers about to launch against the Syrian aircraft. I suspect we would have been next on the hit parade."

It was that reasoning that had earlier given Lord the

one argument, his only argument, when he reported up the chain of command.

"Have you contacted the JCs?" Sacrette was turning slightly; locked at attention, he was watching Lord, who was standing at the coaming, staring out at the sea. The question made Lord's shoulders hunch up, as though someone had punched him in the spine.

"Not yet. I was waiting for your report and for confirmation from the Syrian commander at Al Ladhiqyah. Then, and only then, I'll report to the JCs."

Before he could say another word, Captain Opsta exploded onto the bridge. "You better hear this, admiral. All hell's busting loose in Baghdad."

"Baghdad! My God, the shit's already hitting the fan." Lord looked like a man being led to the gallows as he walked into the CIC, followed by the three pilots.

In the CIC, Lt. Tim Polson, one of the communication officers fluent in Arabic, rose and slammed the palm of his hand against his computer console. "Holy Jesus, admiral. You gotta listen to this. I've got Baghdad radio. Everything's jumping."

Lord's head jerked to the officer. "Settle down, son. What's happening?"

"Sorry, sir, but you better listen to this. The radio waves are really cooking out of Baghdad."

"Jesus, Joseph, and Mary," Lord muttered.

With a flick of his hand, Polson turned on the intercom, sharing the intercepted transmission from the satellite LaCrosse.

LaCrosse, a communications satellite capable of eavesdropping on microwave transmissions, was intercepting communications from throughout the Middle East.

The voice was in Arabic; the speaker's voice was heated, and very fast.

"What's all that gibberish about, Polson?" asked Sacrette.

Polson began translating. "It's President Saddam Hussein. He sounds like he could shit nails, captain."

Hussein's voice then commanded the CIC.

". . . People of Iraq. Your president is safe. Allah has protected me from the treachery of a traitor. This morning, a cowardly terrorist exploded a bomb in one of our military installations. I was not there. The traitor was killed. The matter is being investigated. I speak to you now to dispel the rumors. I am safe, alive, and prepared to defend our land to the death. . . ."

The transmission ended.

"An inside job?" asked Sacrette.

Lord nodded. "An attempt nonetheless. Which means, coupled with the C-130, we better be prepared for the fallout. Launch the Alert Five. Go to Station X-ray."

Station Yankee was a station of full preparedness. Station Zulu was a station of impending attack. Station X-Ray was the station of preparedness where the planes were launched, the guns loaded, and the finger on the trigger.

Across the flight deck boomed the intercom ordering, "Launch the Alert Five."

Within five minutes, four F/A-18 Hornets launched from the waist and bow catapults. Five minutes later, four F-14 Tomcats were then locked into the shuttle and catapulted into the sky above the Mediterranean.

The long-range and short-range punch of the BG was ready to fight a war!

"What about the Herky?" asked Sacrette, referring to the C-130 by its nickname. He had nearly forgotten about the C-130 during the excitement. That was when Captain Opsta handed Admiral Lord a telephone. "The Syrian commander is on the horn, sir."

Lord took the telephone and listened to the Syrian commander's report. After several minutes, his face went ashen. When finished, he hung up the telephone and walked to the bridge.

Sacrette followed, motioning with his head for the younger pilots to find someplace else to go.

"What's the bottom line, sir?" Sacrette leaned on the coaming beside Lord. Looking into the admiral's eyes, he saw sheer confusion.

"The Syrian commander reported there were no survivors."

"How many aboard?"

"Forty-eight, including the pilot and co-pilot."

Sacrette sensed there was more. "It couldn't have been a humanitarian flight, admiral. Humanitarians don't carry Stingers."

Lord shrugged. "Not unless you consider forty-six heavily-armed men wearing freefall parachutes as representatives of humanitarian aid."

The air nearly went out of Sacrette's lungs. "What are you saying, sir?"

"We don't have to worry about the Iraqi government claiming we shot down one of their aircraft. They probably don't know about the aircraft, humanitarian or otherwise. More than likely, the Syrian shot down one of our aircraft loaded with commandos."

10

MAJOR SAM MCGEE WAS STARING THROUGH A HAZE at a face framed in a carpet of thick fur and covered with a turban wound tightly around the head. The man's clothes looked like rags; his smell was remindful of a horse.

When the man spoke, McGee saw something immediately noticeable. His teeth were white, porcelain, perfect, unlike the stained teeth of the old man sitting beside him.

Damned perfect teeth, thought McGee.

"Rest easy, sir. You had a dislocated shoulder. It's been re-set. It'll hurt like bloody hell for a few hours," said the voice in perfect English. Not American English—the real thing—British.

"Who are you?" asked McGee.

"Captain Norwood Cullen Donaldson. British Special Air Service. SAS."

"Well, I'll be damned." said McGee. "I believe the appropriate greeting is Who Dares Wins."

"That's correct, sir."

McGee shifted onto his good side. The room was dark, except for a fire burning in a clay fireplace in the center of what was no more than a hut. "Where am I?"

Donaldson nodded at Suleiman. "We are in this man's home. He found you after the crash."

"What are you doing here?" asked McGee, not sure he wanted to know.

Donaldson shook his head. "That's classified, sir."

McGee understood. "What's the next move?"

Donaldson squatted on the floor. He looked like a man who was accustomed to the environment. He took a Sykes-Fairburn commando knife and drew in the dirt floor. "We're here." He dug a small hole. Then the tip of the blade inched north. "Here's Turkey. We've got to get you to Turkey."

That was when McGee shot upright. A bolt of pain raced from his feet to his head, then back again. "My aircraft!"

Donaldson gently lowered McGee back to the blanket on the floor. Raising a glass of hot tea to McGee's mouth, Donaldson said, "Your aircraft is under cover. My men have it hidden." He chuckled. "A bloody amazing machine. I've never seen one up close."

"Not many have, captain, which is why the aircraft can't be found. Do you understand?" There was an unmistakable urgency in the pilot's voice.

"Yes, sir. My men have the bird wired with enough explosives to bring an entire mountain down on the aircraft. Nobody will get their hands on the stealth. You have my word."

McGee relaxed. With the cloud clearing rapidly from his head, the pieces were starting to fall into place. He was beginning to figure out the SAS's presence. "SAS. British commandos. You boys are mostly anti-terrorist specialists."

Donaldson nodded. "Yes, sir."

McGee remembered another aspect of the elite fighting unit's special mission. "And hostage rescue."

Donaldson said nothing. He merely grinned, then asked, "What happened to you, sir? Were you shot down?"

McGee shook his head. "As you Brits say, 'bloody bad run of luck.' I flew through some kind of firestorm over Baghdad, some kind of explosion. Debris punctured my engines. I was making for my alternate at Adana, Turkey, but the fans quit on me a few miles from here."

Donaldson thought for a moment. "Did you say there was an explosion?"

"That's right. I was flying over the city center at about two hundred feet, right down their throat. Suddenly, the sky in front of me lit up like the fourth of July. Hell of an explosion."

"What were you doing flying over Baghdad at that altitude?"

Now it was McGee's chance to grin. A grin that said, "Ask me no questions, I'll tell you no lies. . . ."

Donaldson seemed to understand. "There are reports some bloke tried to kill President Hussein. Blew up one of the operation centers Hussein uses as a hideout. The bugger is moving around like Khadafi now that some of his own people want him dead."

"Were they successful?"

Donaldson looked disappointed. "No. He's alive."

"Thank God," said McGee. "That might send the balloon up."

Donaldson shrugged. "Quite possible."

McGee slowly rose to his feet. "Can you radio my people and let them know I'm safe?"

"We already have."

"And?"

"We're arranging a STAR snatch."

"Jesus." McGee swallowed hard. "That's not my idea of a fun trip to Turkey."

"Beats the hell out of walking, sir."

Donaldson had a menacing twinkle in his eye. McGee figured the SAS soldier had ridden the STAR, surface-to-air-rescue, before. McGee had done it once. Harnessed to a tethered gas-filled balloon, a C-130 flies low, retrieves the balloon and snatches the harnessed subject off the ground. A wild ride follows while the subject is winched into the cargo hold of the C-130.

Helluva ride.

"When?"

"They'll airdrop the STAR at 2000 hours, we'll hook you up, and the extract aircraft will come at 2030 hours."

"At night?"

"Yes, sir. It'll be a memorable evening."

Before McGee could add his thoughts on the situation, a burly, flat-faced man entered the hut. "We've got Iraqi soldiers on the road, sir," he said with a British accent.

"Christ." Donaldson was up and moving through the narrow door. Following close behind, McGee knew it wasn't the time for questions. it was time to follow and do whatever he was instructed.

"Put this on. Quickly." Donaldson gave McGee a heavy goatskin coat and old trousers. The flat-faced man began wrapping a turban around the pilot's head. McGee wanted to shout from the pain in his shoulder but said nothing. Instead, he stood trembling, trying to ignore the pain as the SAS soldiers tried to turn him from a black American fighter pilot into a Kurdish goat herder.

Minutes later, an Iraqi truck roared into the tiny village. Six soldiers piled out and began walking around, stretching, carrying their weapons on their shoulders as though they were shovels.

Seated on the ground in a circle, McGee sat between Donaldson and Suleiman. Across from the pilot sat other Kurds; their eyes were aflame with the hatred they felt for the Iraqi soldiers.

An Iraqi officer stepped into the circle and jutted out his hand. The Kurds seemed to understand. They produced identity cards. Donaldson produced an identity card.

McGee felt his stomach tighten. The officer, short and dumpy in appearance, kicked McGee in the side. "Your identity card!"

McGee looked at Donaldson, whose sun-bronzed face leered from beneath the turban. As the officer kicked again, McGee jerked, not noticing Donaldson stare past the men in the circle to the hut.

He nodded ever so slightly.

A storm of muffled coughs broke the air surrounding the circle. From the narrow doorways of the huts, round cylindrical barrels spit a momentary flame of red fire, then fell silent as smoke wafted from the barrels.

The six Iraqi soldiers died instantly. The officer pitched backward into a small goat pen. He lay in a pile of manure, his eyes staring up to the sky. Above his eyes, a round hole oozed a thin trail of blood.

"Let's move!" Donaldson shouted.

From the huts, five men, including the flat-faced Brit, suddenly appeared, dressed in Kurdish clothing. Each wore the same hardened look as Donaldson.

Each gripped a smoking automatic pistol equipped with a silencer.

11

1600.

SCUTTLEBUTT ABOARD AN AIRCRAFT CARRIER MOVES along the grapevine with extraordinary speed. The arrival of two intelligence officers from the United Nations multinational force turned the grapevine into a sizzling wire of speculation and expectation.

CPO Desmond "Diamonds" Farnsworth was the maintenance chief of the VFA-101 Hornets fighter attack squadron. A burly, muscular, black man, his shaved scalp always seemed to bear a thin cap of sweat. When his eyes narrowed, face furrowed, and the skin of his forehead pushed down on the bridge of his nose, he looked like a bulldog ready to snap.

Scuttlebutt was one of the irritations that brought about this particular facial characteristic, a characteristic his men recognized, one that meant put a lid on your lip and get back to work.

If there was any new "skinny," as the "word" was

called, Diamonds knew the chiefs would know before the enlisted men, or so he thought. To be certain he went to the best source of intel aboard the *Valiant* to learn first hand.

Sacrette was coming out of his office on the hangar deck when Diamonds caught up with the CAG.

"Thunderbolt," Diamonds shouted over the din.

Sacrette appeared in a hurry. "What can I do for you in a few short seconds, chief? I'm headed for a briefing."

Diamonds pulled up short. Something is happening, he told himself. "The grapevine's jumping with some new word. Says there's a couple of desert rats on board. What's going on?"

Sacrette shrugged. "Your guess is as good as mine." He winked. "I'll let you know in a bit. Meanwhile, roll Commander Riendeau's E-2 onto the flight deck. He'll be departing at 1830."

Diamonds nodded. E-2—the Hawkeye AWACs aircraft. Must be something happening.

Sacrette made his way below to the VFA-101 ready room. The plush, carpeted room filled with leather chairs was empty except for Admiral Lord and two officers.

One was a Brit, a colonel. He wore a powder-blue beret; on the beret was a pin bearing a sword superimposed over a pair of wings. SAS.

The second was an American. He wore a green camouflage utility cap. On the cap was the rank insignia of a commander and the gold badge of the Navy SEALs.

Lord introduced the men. "Colonel Dillon, British SAS. Commander Mattern, SEAL Team Two. This is the commander of the air wing, Captain Sacrette."

Sacrette shook hands, then eased into a chair. Lord nodded to Mattern.

"Captain Sacrette, we have a joint British-American covert operation currently underway in the area of operation." Sacrette knew the AO was considered Kuwait and Iraq.

"I'm listening."

Mattern continued. "Colonel Dillon and I are the operational coordinators of Operation Desert Star. Elements of SEAL Team Two and one Red Cell team are scheduled for deployment in Kuwait City. Their mission is to provide military assistance to a Kuwaiti resistance movement currently being organized in the city."

"In the event the U.N. forces go to war with Iraq." It was a statement, not a question.

"Correct." Mattern continued. "The teams are to contact a local resistance leader who has established an underground network. The mission is twofold: first, to pinpoint locations where foreigners are being held as 'shields' in the event of an attack. Second, to organize the resistance into a viable guerilla force in the event of conflict."

Sacrette grimaced. The cowardly act of using foreign "guests"—as Saddam Hussein termed the hostages—was one of the key factors preventing an all-out military operation against Iraq. "Do you know how many hostages are still inside Kuwait?"

Mattern shrugged. "Not precisely. As you know, the women and children have been allowed to leave. That still leaves the men. By knowing their exact location we may be able to save many of them in the event of an all-out military operation."

"Is an all-out military operation planned?"

Mattern shook his head emphatically. "There are several contingency plans, captain, but only contingencies.

In the event of such an operation our people will be on the inside."

Sacrette looked at Dillon. "What's the British part in this?"

Dillon explained. "SAS teams are inside Iraq with a similar mission—organizing resistance movements, plotting locations of the 'guests,' and preparing for harassment and interdiction measures in the event of war."

Sacrette looked quickly at Admiral Lord. "Christ. The C-130. Were those SAS troops aboard that Herky?"

Dillon answered the question. "We know about the Hercules. They were not part of any multi-national force, covert or otherwise."

"Who were they?" Sacrette wondered aloud.

"There's no way of knowing," Lord answered. "The bodies bore no identification. What remained was unidentifiable. I'm afraid it's a mystery. But one thing is certain—they weren't friendlies."

Relieved, Sacrette spoke to Mattern. There was no hiding his thoughts. "What you're doing is risky."

Mattern grumped. "These are risky times."

Sacrette considered the operation. Desert Star seemed necessary. It appeared logical, but there was still a matter to discuss. He looked at Mattern. "Where do we come in, commander? Requesting the commander of the air wing to fly a covert mission behind enemy lines is not only questionable, it's damned suspicious."

A long pause followed. "Aside from the on-going operation, there's another matter of urgency. We have been requested by the royal family to assist in the extraction of one remaining member of the Sabah family still inside Kuwait. Prince Ali Ben Sabah."

Sacrette breathed heavily. He recognized the name of

the man considered the favorite nephew of the emir of Kuwait. "That's why you're sending in a Red Cell team. You're not taking any chances."

"Our contact with the resistance group has sheltered Prince Sabah in a safe location. However, the situation in Kuwait City is quite fluid. Things change very quickly. Prince Sabah is running out of time. In exchange for the resistance leader's cooperation, we have to bring out the prince. The Sabah family is pushing hard from the other end in Washington."

"What do you have in mind?" Sacrette asked.

Mattern spread a map of the area onto a table. "We keep it simple. An aircraft will deploy to this point." Mattern touched an isolated area of the Kuwaiti desert. "This is an oasis. You'll be met by the contact. The contact will get you inside the city. You and elements of SEAL Team Two and the Red Cell team will infiltrate to the part of the city where the prince and his family are hiding. You and the Red Cell team will bring the prince and his family out. SEAL Two will stay with the resistance."

"Why not simply have the contact bring the prince to the deployment point?" asked Sacrette.

Mattern shook his head. "Like I said, these are risky times, but that's too risky. There are children and an elderly woman. Getting a whole group of people through the checkpoints would be impossible."

Sacrette's mouth tightened for a moment, then relaxed as he realized something important. "You want me to fly the helo."

Mattern looked at Dillon, then to Lord. Finally, he leaned over the table, staring squarely into Sacrette's blue eyes. "No, captain. The mission doesn't call for the use of a helo. The range is too far. Instead, we will be using an Osprey."

Sacrette was qualified in the vertical-take-off-landing (VTOL) aircraft that was part helo, part transport plane. "I can handle the Osprey, along with a dozen other pilots in the navy. Which brings us back to my question: what do you want from me?"

"We don't want you to fly the Osprey. We want you to lead the extraction team. The leader of the resistance is being very cagey. Smart like a fox. He won't give the contact the whereabouts of the Sabah family in the event the contact is captured by the Iraqis."

"How the hell are we supposed to know the Sabah family's location?"

Mattern smiled softly. "Apparently, you already know the location of the Sabah family. The leader of the resistance said you would understand."

"Me?"

"Yes. He sent a courier through Iraqi lines two nights ago. The courier was carrying an item he said was meant for you."

"What item?"

Mattern reached to his pocket and removed a metal badge which he lay on the table.

Sacrette stared at the badge for a moment. A fond smile spread across his lips. He picked it up. The badge was Iranian pilot wings. Pilot wings worn by royal air force pilots during the reign of the Shah. Turning the wings over, he found what he expected to find. On the back were the initials MRM.

"Do you recognize those initials, captain?" Colonel Dillon asked.

Sacrette nodded, then whispered, "The wings belong

to an old friend of mine. A former pilot in the Royal Iranian Air Force. Mohammad Reza Mostafavi."

"Then you'll do it?" asked Mattern.

Sacrette was quick to consent; there was no hesitation. He knew Mostafavi wouldn't leave him dangling on a meat hook. "I'll do it. But we will need to make a few changes."

"What kind of changes?" asked Mattern. He sounded cautious.

Sacrette explained. When finished, the two commando leaders looked at the CAG incredulously.

Dillon spoke first, more a rush of words than a statement. "You're insane!"

Sacrette grinned. "No, colonel. It's the quickest, most expeditious way to pull this off. Besides, the Iraqis won't suspect something like this in a thousand years."

After giving Sacrette's request some thought, Mattern nailed down the operation.

"You'll have what you want."

12

CPO Farnsworth was closing the radome on an F/A-18 Hornet when Sacrette approached. Seeing that Sacrette look of mischief he had come to recognize in their more than twenty-year relationship, he waited expectantly for the CAG to speak.

"We have a mission, chief."

Farnsworth wiped his hands on a rag. "You had to come down here to tell me that, sir?"

Sacrette knew when he was caught out by the chief. He shook his head. "No. What I have to say needs to be said at eyeball level."

Farnsworth nodded to the upper deck. "The desert rats?"

Sacrette nodded, then added quickly, "An old friend of ours is in a tight situation."

"Who's the old friend?"

"Mohammad Mostafavi."

"Let's get some chow. You can fill me in while we eat. I suspect it might be a while before we get home cooking."

The two sailors walked toward the elevator while Sacrette explained. "Mohammad is hiding members of the royal family in Kuwait City. He won't divulge the location. Got any hunches?"

Farnsworth thought for a moment. "During Operation War Chariot, you sent me to his shop. Mohammad took me into a secret room in the back, a room that was more like a bunker. It was hidden behind a wall panel. Steel doors, humidity controlled—a giant walk-in safe complete with living quarters. He had enough weapons in there to start a war."

Sacrette knew Mostafavi was an arms dealer as well as a coin dealer. He was also a man who planned for the future. "That safe of his is bomb resistant and fireproof."

"Are you thinking what I'm thinking?"

"I'll bet three months pay the royal family is in the safe."

"That'll be a good bet." Diamonds paused. "What do you want from me, Thunderbolt?"

Sacrette shrugged. "Back-up insurance. If something happens to me, you know the location. Just as important—Mohammad knows you."

There was no hesitation in Diamonds' reply. "When do we leave?"

Sacrette checked his watch. "Thirty minutes."

Diamonds grinned. "Let's rock and roll."

"I'll meet you on the flight deck. Be suited up."

Diamonds forgot about going to the mess hall, but

there was one thing he needed to know. "Where's the operational platform?"

"Saudi Arabia. An airbase in the desert. Al Salamiyah."

Diamonds laughed. "Sounds like an Italian love song."

13

Abu Dhabi, United Arab Emirates.
0015.

ALI AKHBAR MURJAN WAS WORKING HIS PRAYER BEADS through his fingers while sitting in a rococo-style chair in a high-rise penthouse overlooking the old, high-walled fort of Shakhbut. Murjan, the Iranian minister of the interior, a position that was merely a cover for his true work as director of Iran's terrorist network, spoke with a gravelly voice that was nothing more than a whisper. Himself a victim of counter-terrorism from the Mossad in 1984, Murjan had opened a diplomatic pouch containing a copy of the Koran, which exploded, blowing away an ear, half of the terrorist's face, and nearly destroying his larynx.

Murjan, a forty-two-year-old senior mullah, was not only evil in his heart, he was evil in his appearance. Dressed in a dark turban and dark robe, his aura was menacing, intimidating.

Sitting across from Murjan, Sheik Mohammad Shehab felt his skin crawl as he listened to the voice that seemed to rise up from the stomach. Disappointment was on his face, disappointment from hearing a situation report that was even more difficult to accept.

"The aircraft carrying one group of our men was shot down after crossing the Syrian border. My sources report there were no survivors."

For the first time since Murjan's arrival, an hour ago from Shiraz, in Iran, Shehab expressed relief. "At least, the Syrians will not be able to conduct an interrogation."

Murjan flipped his beads nonchalantly. "It was the last group, Group Six. The plane would not have been approached except for the United Nation's embargo authorized yesterday morning. It was unpredictable. The will of Allah."

Shehab's eyes widened in astonishment. "Let us pray Allah's will causes no more complications. Those men had an important assignment, one that was critical to the success of our plan. How will they be replaced?"

In his slow, deliberate manner, Murjan tried to calm the sheik. "They will not be replaced."

"Each group has a specific mission, each mission an integral part of the whole. We are gambling with success. That is not a gamble I wish to make. This is the second failure in one day. First, the attempt on Hussein. Now, the loss of the men aboard the Hercules."

Murjan settled the sheik. "The plan will be successful. The attempt on Hussein was always marginal in its success projection. Killing a head of state is not something one can guarantee. No matter. The message is still there: there *was* an attempt! That may be more powerful than his death. He is still in charge and will act impulsively, not with calculation."

"Yes, but Group Six was important."

"No need for concern. The remaining elements will carry out their tasks. They will be sufficient. Once in place, the signal will be sent, then the two-headed devil will begin devouring its own flesh."

Shehab clapped his hands together as though trying to chase away the doubt. "The world will shake. The two great armies will collide. War will erupt almost instantly."

"Yes, as planned. The Iraqis will believe the United States has launched an attack. They will attack the American troops in Saudi Arabia. The oil fields will be the first targets. Initially, the oil fields and refineries in Kuwait will be destroyed, from Rikkah to Mina Saud, either by American bombers or by the Iraqis themselves. The Iraqis will attack the Saudi oil fields and refineries throughout Saudi Arabia. The Americans will attack the oil fields in Iraq. The bombers from American aircraft carriers are only a few minutes from the Iraqi oil fields and refineries around Basra. Fifty percent of the world's oil-producing fields and refineries will be destroyed."

Shehab nearly choked at the possibilities that would then exist. "The price of oil will skyrocket beyond belief. With the three largest oil producers out of business in the Persian Gulf, our cartel will reap enormous wealth."

"That is the agreement. My network has supplied the method. Your cartel will provide the necessary assistance to my government."

"But, of course, according to our agreement, our cartel will finance the rebuilding of Iran's oil producing capability."

Murjan's mouth parted into a mysterious smile. "That is the plan. Our oil in Iran will have greater value. More importantly, our two greatest enemies—Iraq and America—will begin the slow process of bleeding each other to death in the sand."

14

0030.

McGee knew the emotion of fear was the most powerful to overcome from having faced fear a thousand times. Fear was personal, private, but manageable, so long as it was kept in perspective. Situational awareness, SA, was what fighter pilots used to overcome their fear. Retaining awareness gave one confidence in any situation, especially in the cockpit, for that was the private, personal world of the fighter pilot.

Outside the cockpit was different, SA was reduced to the elements. Gone now was the swagger, the arrogance, even the cockiness. He couldn't see what lay in the darkness below, but he knew there was nothing but air beyond his fingertips, air that extended downward for several thousand feet. A sheer drop.

And he was supposed to sleep!

Donaldson and the other SAS soldiers had roped their bodies to a single carabiner driven into the face of a sheer rock cliff overlooking a valley split by the Tigris. McGee couldn't see the river, but he could hear the roar and knew it was there.

"Where are we going?" he had asked.

"South," Donaldson said simply.

"What about the STAR snatch?"

Donaldson had looked off to the sun as it was nearing the horizon and shrugged. "Too late, mate. You're with us now, get that in your head. We'll try to get you to your people, but our mission comes first. Consider yourself as SAS."

McGee didn't ask about the SAS mission. He knew that would be futile. The SAS officer's lips were tighter than a frog's ass underwater when it came to discussing their operational plan. He remembered thinking that sometimes it was best not to know where you were going.

What he wasn't counting on was the route. A large mountain stood in their way. Sheer rock, straight up.

Christ!

So he climbed the mountain while being pulled up by the soldiers who scaled the face as though they were salamanders. Strong, sturdy fingers gripped fissures; feet skillfully perched, the lead climber drove a piton into the rock while perched over oblivion, then he would thread his lifeline through the eyelet, and start upward again.

Looking out toward the blackness, McGee saw the stars twinkling. They seemed to be directly across from him. He started to reach and touch a star, then withdrew his hand as though fearing to touch something hot.

Finally, he screamed. A loud scream that echoed and reverberated through his skull but never passed through his lips.—*Where are we going?*

Al Salamiyah.
0100.

QUONSET HUTS CIRCLED THE AIRSTRIP AT AL SALAMIYAH, near Riyadh, sitting like large oil drums half buried in the sand. Surrounded by sandbagged gun emplacements, the Quonsets served as quick-to-erect hangars to house dozens of fighter craft. In the Quonset hangar where he had just parked his F/A-18, Sacrette recognized the voice before he saw the face.

"Thunderbolt!"

A group of twenty-four men approached. Each man carried heavy duffel bags and an array of weapons ranging from Uzi's to the more specialized varieties, including crossbows, sniper rifles, and ultralight automatic weapons and shotguns.

SEALs.

The baddest boys on the block, or so thought Sacrette, who had worked with the navy's special ops units before.

At the lead was an old friend. Lieutenant Commander John "Breaker" LeDuc was short and barrel-chested with a menacing smile. The tough and rugged Red Cell Four team commander swaggered toward Sacrette with his hand extended. Dressed in desert camouflage, he was followed closely by his five men, all sailors and equally tough looking in character and presence.

The Red Cell teams were an ultra-secretive unit; each team was composed of six men drawn from within the SEALs. A hostage rescue counter-terrorist unit, the Red Cell teams were called on to perform tasks similar to their British counterparts, the SAS.

The remaining SEALs were men of Seal Team Two stationed in Little Creek, Virginia.

"You're looking fit, John. The desert must appeal to you." Sacrette tapped LeDuc's hardened stomach. The SEAL commander's face was so deeply tanned, his skin was nearly the color of honey.

"This goddamned country is hot, captain. Hotter'n a whore's breath."

Sacrette laughed as he introduced CPO Farnsworth. LeDuc looked angularly at Diamonds. "Farnsworth? Do you have a son named Daniel?"

Diamonds grinned. "Yes, sir. He's with Force Recon. He wanted to be a jarhead."

LeDuc nodded. "We went to the naval academy together. He's a good marine."

Sacrette glanced at the five men with LeDuc. "Your boys?"

LeDuc introduced the men of Red Cell Four: the exec was Lieutenant Steve Lipp, a muscular, young man who carried a rifle case. Sacrette suspected the rifle was sniper-designed with an infrared scope and silencer. Around his neck was a wire saw, which had become something of a trademark among the men of the navy's six active Red Cell teams.

The four remaining members of RC 4 were enlisted personnel, all professional military men.

Bruce "Doc" Valance, the team medic, was carrying a SAW machinegun. His specialty, besides medicine, was heavy weapons.

Trinidad "Trini" Caisson was from Puerto Rico, a tough-looking character with a long scar across his cheek. Strapped to his forearm was a Sykes-Fairburn commando fighting knife. Sacrette figured this was the man who handled the "wet" situations.

Brooks Bollinger was the demolitions expert. He was a muscular kid with reddish-brown hair, dancing eyes, and an easy gait. On his shoulder he carried a heavy rucksack.

Last was a black man, thin, rangy, with a face that looked like it was carved from granite. Jessie "Bingo" Starr was the team recon expert.

Sacrette looked past LeDuc and RC4 at the men from SEAL Team Two. "Where's the commanding officer from SEAL Two?"

"His name is Commander Brad Davies. Davies is in ops talking with a civilian type from DIA."

Sacrette looked at Diamonds. "Get them loaded, chief. We'll go find Davies."

Sacrette, followed by LeDuc and Lipp, started for the operations center in the main terminal building of the airport.

"What in the hell is DIA doing here?" Sacrette wondered aloud.

"Scuttlebutt has it one of the air force's bird's has gone down. A stealth fighter."

Sacrette stopped cold in his tracks. He had been the training officer during the FY-117A's carrier landing training phase. The FY-117A was the air force's only "carrier capable" aircraft, and its pilots the only air force pilots trained in carrier landings.

Sacrette knew most of the pilots and had even flown the stealth fighter himself.

"Where did the bird go down.?"

LeDuc said nothing. He just nodded toward the north.

"Damn." Sacrette shook his head. What was puzzling him was why the DIA was talking to the SEALs.

That was when something else made sense: The ident from a locator that LaCrosse had received.

16

Aaron Feinberg wasn't in the ops center; he was in the hangar where two stealth fighters sat draped in heavy camouflage netting. A portable computer center was stationed beneath the wing of one stealth. The screen was projecting the beacon signature from the downed stealth.

There was a second signature on the screen, one the KH-12 had been required to tune into a special frequency in order to receive.

Commander Brad Davies, a tall, hulking SEAL, was listening to Feinberg explain the second signature. "There's a small, pill-shaped transmitter implanted beneath the skin of McGee's left armpit. A similar implant is worn by all stealth fighter pilots. Aside from those pilots, similar transmitters are worn by only a few, all civilians, except for the chairman of the Joint Chiefs of Staff, and the president of the United States."

"Whatever is happening, he's moving," Davies said while sipping coffee. He was staring at the signature over the rim of a styrofoam cup when Sacrette approached with Lipp and LeDuc.

Looking at Sacrette, Feinberg snapped, "This is a classified area, captain. You and your men are not authorized to be in here."

Sacrette stopped abruptly, then ignored the admonishment as he walked to one of the stealth fighters. He ran his hand along the leading edge of the wing. "My name's Sacrette. I'm the CAG from Battle Group Zulu Station."

Feinberg nodded knowingly. "I was about to send for you, captain."

"Oh? For what purpose?"

Feinberg pointed to the computer screen. "One of our pilots is down inside Iraqi territory. For some reason, he's on the move."

"Captured by the Iraqis?"

Feinberg shook his head. "That was my first impression, but not any longer. The signal we're getting from him clearly indicates he's moving, moving slow, a broken pattern. And, more than likely, he's on foot."

Sacrette understood. "If the Iraqis had picked him up, the pilot would be on the fastest available transport to Baghdad so Hussein could hold a press conference."

"That's right."

"Which one of your boys went down?"

"Captain McGee."

"Sam McGee?"

"You know him." It wasn't a question.

Sacrette's eyes looked momentarily pained. "I was his training officer during the wing's carrier landing phase. He's a damn good pilot."

Feinberg's face was nearly pressed against the screen. "Yes. A damn good pilot."

"Why were you going to send for me?" Sacrette asked.

Feinberg pointed at the ident signature of the downed stealth fighter. "I have a problem, one that takes precedence over any mission you might have at the moment, including your mission into Kuwait. Frankly, I need your help. This is strictly voluntary, but your present assets have temporarily been assigned to my authority." He was looking at the SEALs.

Sacrette's eyes narrowed. "What in the hell do you mean, your 'authority'?"

Feinberg didn't look or sound apologetic. He spoke in no uncertain terms. "I've received approval from the Joint Chiefs to assume control of your SEAL and aircraft assets." He handed Sacrette a computer printout.

The order was from the chairman, instructing Captain Sacrette to assist DIA representative Feinberg.

"Of course, this doesn't include you as a part of the mission. Once *my* mission is complete, you can continue with *your* mission in Kuwait, but I believe you can be of major importance to this operation."

Sacrette stood there for a moment looking foolish. Finally, his curiosity and sense of military priority took command. "What do you have in mind, Mr. Feinberg?"

Feinberg went to an operational map of Iraq. He pointed at a symbol denoting an airbase. "You fly to Damascus, then east to the Syrian airbase at Palmyre where you refuel. After refueling, you and the SEALs will cross into Iraq and conduct a two-prong operation. First, you make certain the stealth is secured, especially the electronics pod in the bomb bay, it's a highly classified piece of technology. We don't want anyone—repeat—anyone, to get their hands on that pod."

"What about the stealth fighter itself?"

"Destroy the stealth. Don't leave a scrap of the fighter for anyone to find."

Sacrette appeared stunned. "Christ, Feinberg, when you go, you go all the way, don't you, sir?"

"Problems?"

"Hell, yes. Quite a few. First—why me?"

"Several reasons. One, among other assets such as the SEALs and Osprey, your file says you're a bronco, which means you've got a pair of balls, not to mention you're already on the move with a Red Cell team and a contingent from Seal Team Two. That puts you several jumps ahead of organizing a new mission team. Second, you know the area. I understand your aircraft went down inside Iraq in 1974 when you were a training advisor for the Shah's air force. Is that correct?"

Sacrette nodded slowly. "Yes, sir. I went down in the north, not far from where the stealth is located. I was found by Kurds. They treated me well and led me across the border into Turkey."

"Precisely. Those Kurds could become quite useful in recovering the stealth."

Sacrette sensed there was more. "Is that it?"

Feinberg shook his head. "There's the matter of McGee. I don't know what's happening, but we don't want him captured by the Iraqis. I want him found and brought out." Feinberg looked at LeDuc. "That'll be your mission, commander. We can guide you to his location. Recover McGee and bring him home. McGee, the stealth, and/or the electronics pod. Destroy the stealth if necessary, but recover the pod."

Sacrette studied the map. "Getting in and out won't be easy. The Iraqis are on full alert."

Feinberg waved off the notion. "The Iraqis have all eyes and ears trained on the south. Besides, I've seen the Osprey. I know what you have in mind. We can run a jamming operation by satellite on Iraqi tracking facilities. You'll slip in and out, avoiding terrain at low level."

"Which raises the next question," said Sacrette. "What about the royal family in Kuwait?"

"When the stealth operation is concluded, you'll deploy to Dharan. You can rescue the royal family from there. They take second fiddle to the stealth and McGee."

Sacrette hated the thought, but knew Feinberg was right. The fighter and pilot were too important. That left one matter for Sacrette. "Where is the Osprey?"

Feinberg laughed. "I understand there was a rush job, but it's ready, per your request. Come with me."

"What about the digital map displays of Iraq?" asked Sacrette. He knew the map would be important.

"The computer has already been programmed with the software."

Sacrette looked at the three junior officers. "Gentlemen, let's climb aboard."

Following Feinberg, the four officers entered an adjacent Quonset. Diamonds and the men from Seal Two were already loaded.

Parked in the hangar was an MV-22 Osprey. The multi-role transport was designed to carry nearly fifty troops into combat from a variety of locations. Terrain and takeoff roll were no problem; the Osprey, a VTOL aircraft, could takeoff and land either conventionally or vertically.

"Hell of an idea, captain." Diamonds was standing in front of the Osprey.

Sacrette grinned at the aircraft, which sat painted in the markings of the *Al Quwwat al Jawwiya al Iraqiya:* the Iraqi air force.

PART TWO: INFILTRATORS

17

Kuwait City.
0500.

MOHAMMAD MOSTAFAVI KNELT IN THE DARKNESS; sweat trickled down his face, stinging his eyes, eyes he couldn't dare wipe. Movement at this moment would mean death, so he stared at the soft, ember glow from two cigarettes burning less than ten feet away by the front door of his shop. Rather, what was once the front door.

He was kneeling behind the only glass counter remaining in the shop. The expensive counters that survived the invasion were on their way to Baghdad, along with much of Mostafavi's inventory, including rare coins, gold plates, and silver ingots—a fortune. But he still had the inventory that was cached away in the secret wall-safe in the rear. He was pleased the safe had not been found by the Iraqis. Then again, he wasn't surprised.

The Iraqis weren't very smart at finding things that weren't in front of their noses.

Sliding along the floor, he closed his eyes to the darting pain from slivers of glass pricking the palms of his hands. He kept his eyes on the two soldiers, watching their backs as their silhouettes remained framed against the thin veil of moonlight coming in from where a window once stood.

Carefully, he crept along the floor until he was close enough to smell the pungent smoke from their cigarettes.

One soldier laughed softly. He was telling the other about a Kuwaiti caught with his four young daughters.

Mostafavi didn't laugh. There was no humor in what he heard.

For the soldiers, there was no humor in what Mostafavi did.

Rising up, Mostafavi placed a pistol near the ear of one soldier and pulled the trigger. The bullet tore through the first soldier's head, exited from the opposite ear, and proceeded through the skull of the second soldier. There was not a sound, except for the muffled cough and the splat of brains and bone slapping against the wall from the silenced .45-caliber projectile.

He caught their bodies, pulled them into a corner, then stripped their weapons and webbing.

"*Allahu akhbar,*" he whispered.

18

CAPTAIN MOSHIN MAGREEB, CHIEF OF THE PALACE guard was sitting near the heavy, steel door sealing the walk-in safe when he heard the hum, then the slight vibration as the vertical locking pins holding the door closed were suddenly freed. The door swung open and Mostafavi slipped through the momentary crack with the speed of a cat.

Closing the door behind him, Mostafavi wiped his hands on a handkerchief.

Magreeb saw the blood. His right eyebrow lifted inquisitively. "Problems?"

Mostafavi shook his head. "Wet work." He was grinning as he stacked the two Iraqi rifles in the corner.

Magreeb, a short, stocky Arab, raised a MAC-10. "What about the Americans? Do you think they will come? I'm starting to have my doubts."

"The Americans will come. I'm certain. We must be patient."

Magreeb's mouth tightened. "I am a soldier. My loyalty is to my emir and my country. I never doubt the wisdom of their words, or their decisions. But now, I have a great fear the prince may have erred. He believes you can get him and his family out of Kuwait. I am no longer certain."

"Your honesty is respected, captain. But the Americans will come."

"We must be prepared for the worst: What if they don't? We're running out of time. The Iraqis will eventually find this place."

Mostafavi knew he was right. Time *was* running out. "Before that happens, we will cross the desert," Mostafavi grunted.

Magreeb seemed to like this idea better than waiting. To wait meant the greater threat of capture. At least, he thought, in the desert we would die like Arabs!

"I must speak to the prince," said Mostafavi, who was pulling back the carpet; a trap door was in the concrete floor. Pulling on a ring, the door opened upward. Quickly, he went down a metal ladder.

The space beneath the safe was nearly the size of his shop. There were four rooms, a small bathroom, an area for cooking, and two bedrooms. The walls were lined with heavy, steel gun lockers.

A sergeant in the palace guard greeted Mostafavi as he came down the ladder.

He went to the last room and knocked lightly on the door.

The door swung open slowly; a dim light bled through

the crack. From inside the room, the outline of a shadow danced eerily off the wall.

"Is it time to leave?" Mostafavi was asked. Jazira Sabah stepped through the door. Her long, black hair hung past her shoulders. Unlike Saudi women, Kuwaiti women had more freely adopted western dress, preferring to shed the purdah—the veil—and let the world see their mysterious beauty. Her large, oval eyes were set within soft, delicate features; she wore Levi's and a T-shirt of her alma mater: Harvard.

Inside, Mostafavi found Jazira's cousin, Prince Ali Ben Sabah. Unlike most of the Sabah princes, Ali chose not to flee in the early hours of the invasion. As a tank commander, he had met the Iraqis as the invading troops pushed into the city and routed the small Kuwaiti army. Driven underground, he had been able to bring his mother, niece, and cousin to Mostafavi, whom he had known since the Iranian arrived in Kuwait.

It was Mostafavi who sent word through the lines that the prince was safely hidden. Fearing the prospect the prince might be captured, thus enhancing the "guest list" of Saddam Hussein, the emir approached the American government to assist in getting Ali out of Kuwait.

Ali was a heavyset man, robust in nature, with flashing, dark eyes, eyes now showing the fatigue and stress of living the life of the pursued.

What Mostafavi saw most was the shame, the identical shame he had felt when he was forced to flee his country with the snapping dogs of tyrants at his heels.

What Ali saw in Mostafavi was disappointment, and the sense of fear that follows failure, or the thought that one's promises might not be kept.

Ali touched Mostafavi's hand lightly. It was an uncommon gesture for royalty. "No matter what happens, my family is in your debt."

Mostafavi shook his head. "The Americans will get you out of Kuwait."

19

0600.

"TIME TO MOVE, MATE, BUT WATCH THAT FIRST STEP. It's a bloody long fall." Captain Donaldson's head peered from inside his sleeping bag. He was looking down the face of the cliff.

"What about room service?" McGee said jokingly, watching the officer as he slipped from inside his sleeping bag like a moth working free of the cocoon. Once free, he leaned out, held to the face by the rope and harness secured by a carabiner to a piton driven into the rock.

Looking around, McGee watched the other SAS soldiers follow Donaldson's lead. Each man carefully, but quickly, rolled his sleeping bag and placed it on his rucksack while dangling on the sheer face of the mountainous wall.

When ready, Donaldson motioned for the lead man to continue. An hour later, the group reached the top.

The force march began without ritual with McGee

placed in the middle. By 1000 the sun was high and the desert heat building. The march was boring with little more to do than walk. And think.

During the march McGee had begun to reconsider the situation.

What had bothered him the most was a purely selfish, but militarily valid point of reasoning: he was important. Damned important. More important was an aircraft any NATO member officer would instantly recognize as being priceless. The last thing the British should want would be for McGee or the stealth to fall into the hands of the Iraqis, for whom the scientific gain would be immeasurable.

Which made him wonder: *Why weren't they doing anything about extracting him and arranging for the recovery of the stealth?*

That thought had plagued him since the arrival of the Iraqi soldiers in Suleiman's village. That and other factors: the SAS soldiers were totally out of contact with any other unit. More importantly, what were the Brit commandos doing in one of the most isolated areas of Iraq?

"What about my extraction, captain?" McGee had stepped alongside the officer.

Donaldson shrugged him off. "Our mission is too important, sir."

McGee didn't like the answer. "What exactly is your mission?"

"I've already told you. That's classified."

"Classified, my ass." McGee gripped the officer's shoulder and turned him around. "I want to know where in the hell you're taking me. I don't care about your mission. I've been plotting the route of our march and we're moving deeper into Iraq. You should certainly be aware of the implications if I'm captured inside Iraq."

Donaldson peeled McGee's fingers from his coat. His eyes suddenly narrowed, turning cold.

"You won't be captured."

McGee pulled back. A smile flashed across his face, then he winked. "You can count on that, slick. I'm going home. You go wherever the hell you want."

McGee started walking north. That's when he heard the metallic ring of a cocking bolt.

McGee turned around. The six Brits had their weapons leveled at his stomach.

"Tie his hands," Donaldson ordered one of the soldiers.

A sickening thought filled McGee's mind, a thought he translated aloud.

"You're not British soldiers."

Donaldson leered at McGee. Gone was the polite air of a British officer trained at Sandhurst.

"You're quite right, Major McGee. We are *former* British soldiers," replied Donaldson.

"What are you now?"

Donaldson smiled, and now it was his turn to wink. "Professional soldiers."

McGee shook his head. "That's just another way of saying you're a fucking mercenary!"

20

Mosul, Iraq.

SUAD SAMARALLAH SLIPPED QUIETLY THROUGH THE streets, being careful not to draw the attention of the soldiers patrolling in the early morning. The sun was starting to rise. The air was chilly, giving a clarity to the voices of the mullahs calling muslims to morning prayers from the minarets spread through the city.

She spit at thinking of the Sunni moslems, defilers of the Koran. The Shi'ite was the true believer. The Shi'ite of the Ayatollah Khomeini. His disciples.

In a rundown, shanty part of town, she slipped through the rear of a small restaurant. The smell of hot coffee filled the air, overpowering the stench of liquor. Liquor was allowed in Iraq, not in Iran. She hated the smell, the taste, but delighted in its use as a weapon.

A weapon she used like her body, knowing Allah would forgive her since she did what she did in his name. Some had become martyrs after death. She had been annointed before becoming a whore in the streets of the city, a whore who squeezed information from soldiers while she drove them to the edge of ecstasy.

She found Latif sipping a thimble of the rich, bitter coffee favored by the Iraqis. She despised its taste, preferring the sweeter blends from South America, which were no longer available.

Suad respected Latif. She didn't know his last name, or if he had one. He was Latif, the mullah who accompanied the Ayatollah to An Najaf after Khomeini was expelled by the Shah in 1963.

When Khomeini went to France, Latif stayed in Iraq, for the Imam had predicted he would one day return to Iran. He predicted he would lead his nation in war against Iraq.

Latif stayed, and built the vast network of espionage and sabotage agents now honeycombed throughout the Middle East. Hezbollah cadre and leadership were Latif's dream, dreams that spawned a nightmare.

Latif was a tall man who walked stooped, a harsh reminder of his treatment from Savak agents in Tehran. He told them nothing, although his fingers were now only twists of meat and bone. The fingernails torn away, he laughed at the army colonel, a colonel he would one day see hanging from a street pole after the prison was stormed.

She stood there, as though waiting for an audience. Reaching to a samovar, he turned the handle and refilled his cup.

"Did you have any trouble, Suad?"

She shook her head. "Nothing a bath won't make me forget."

There was a flicker of sadness in his eyes for a moment.

"Do you have the guard schedule?" He stuck out his hand.

She placed a piece of paper in his upturned palm.

Latif examined the paper. "The officer had much to say in his drunken stupor. Much to say."

"They usually do. The Iraqi soldiers have been drunk on power since taking Kuwait. They finally have much to brag about. I don't think their courage would be so great if it were the Americans they were fighting."

"Quite right. Perhaps you'll see that in the future."

He sat down, then studied her for a moment. Motioning for her to join him, Latif reached into the pocket of his shirt and took out a small packet. She smiled as he handed her the packet of Sanka instant coffee.

"A gift from a friend who arrived last night from Amman." He motioned upward, toward the upstairs bedroom.

Forgetting the coffee, she bolted up the stone stairway leading to the second story of the building.

The stone felt good against her feet; cool, hard, like his body.

She broke through the curtain without stopping and threw herself into his arms.

Khalid Ghani sat upright in the bed. He sat like a prince, framed by the heavy Persian rugs draping the wall. The smell of incense was thick.

Below, Latif could hear her squeels turn to laughter, then her laughter turn to deep groans of passion, like an animal feeding itself on a final meal.

Then his eyes saddened, and he thought of the truth, and realized the accuracy of the thought.

If Allah was benevolent, the lovers would soon feast at His side in Paradise.

21

STANDING ON THE "BUZZARD'S PERCH," THE OBSERVATION platform at the top of the island, Admiral Elrod Lord was wearing his brown aviator's jacket. Dozens of patches were sewn onto the jacket; patches that reminded him of places, airplanes, and men.

And of battle.

These were the lonely moments of battle: a commander forced to stand and wait while his men went into the fray without him. He had to stay at the core of the battle group, directing the fighting flotilla, in many ways, like an orchestra conductor: melded to the baton, never again to draw his bow across the neck of the violin.

Checking his watch, he looked off to the east where the rim of the world was turning golden.

Realizing the battle was soon to be joined, although he fervently hoped it would not, he lightly tapped his briarwood pipe against the railing and went to his own special "pit" to prepare to conduct the scenario.

He found Opsta still at his post in the exec's chair, sipping a can of Coca-Cola and eating a sandwich brought from the mess hall.

"Situation?" asked Lord.

Opsta shook his head. He had a rapport with the admiral; a friendship stretching back through enough years to afford him frankness.

"Not too late to bring them back, Elrod. This mission has made my skin crawl since it began."

"We have our orders. I repeat—what's the situation?"

Opsta's face screwed up like a Pekingese. "On the five yard line and about to cross the goal line."

"Goal line" was the code for the Iraqi border.

"Did Sacrette take on enough fuel?"

"Yes, sir. Enough and then some. Long-range tanks were attached. He can go in, do some sightseeing, and make it back."

The light in the CIC stung Admiral Lord's eyes. He wasn't sure why; he should be used to the soft, red glare after standing in its wash for over two decades. The lines in his face were more like lines in concrete. Not smooth to perfection; not too rough so as appear rugged. Rough—that's what his wife said—he was a man who was rough in appearance.

Inside, he was another kind of man. His wife knew that, too.

He loved his men. His guts now ached and his head throbbed and he could see all their faces as clear as the radar blip approaching the Iraqi border on a nearby radar screen.

"God speed," he whispered.

22

0630.

SACRETTE POINTED THROUGH THE WINDSCREEN OF the twin-engine Osprey. "There's Iraq." In the distance a long pipeline threaded through the desert. To the east lay a majestic mountain range. "The pipeline runs from Shatt al Arab in the Persian Gulf, through the entire length of Iraq, and on into Turkey. It's shut down now on the Turkish side since the invasion." He pointed to the mountains. "The mountains are the Zagros."

"Iran," Farnsworth said into his mouthpiece. He was sitting in the right seat. In the hull the SEALs were sleeping in webbed seats lining the interior.

Not much had been said during the flight from Al Salamiyah. Farnsworth had grabbed a little sleep with Sacrette staying at the controls. The CAG had never been a man requiring much sleep.

He looked down and then said, "We've just crossed into Iraqi territory."

Farnsworth looked out the windscreen. The Osprey was flying approximately ten feet off the ground. "I sure hope there aren't any camels about to stand up down there. If one does, we're dead."

"No sweat, chief." Sacrette punched in the coordinates and felt the inertial guidance system take over the controls. Terrain avoidance was keeping the aircraft a safe height above the ground, which was rough and rugged. The nav system was steering the aircraft toward the signal locating the stealth.

Twenty minutes later Sacrette nudged Farnsworth. "Better get them ready, chief." He nodded toward the windscreen. Two rivers were in plain sight. "The Tigris and the Euphrates, or Al Dijlis and Al Furaat, as they were known during the Mesopotamian period."

The two rivers appeared like silver ribbons, reflecting the early morning sunlight.

Farnsworth pulled himself from his seat and went to where Lipp was sleeping. "Get your boys up, lieutenant. We're inside Iraq."

Wearing the uniform of an Iraqi soldier, Lipp nudged LeDuc.

"Rise and shine," LeDuc barked. Slowly, the SEALs, all dressed in similar uniforms, began to come alive.

"What's our first stop?" Diamonds asked Sacrette as he slid into the right seat in the cockpit.

Sacrette checked the digital map. He touched a point on the map. "A small village called Ishtar. Where I was taken back in 1974, it's Kurdish. The headman is a decent fellow. He hates the Iraqis with a passion."

Diamonds looked suspiciously at Sacrette. "If he's still alive. And, if the village is still there. That's the area where the Iraqis used chemical gas on their own people."

Sacrette had thought of that. "Yeah, the bastards."

"What's the name of the headman?"

Sacrette recalled the Kurd who found him in the mountains and arranged his escape to Turkey.

"A crusty old Kurd. His appearance is enough to scare you to death, but he's a good man. His name is Suleiman Ratab."

What Sacrette wondered most was whether the Kurd was still alive.

23

SULEIMAN RATAB HEARD THE OSPREY WHILE SITTING in his hut. He was boiling tea for his guest, who sat opposite the fire. The guest stiffened at the sound of the incoming aircraft.

"Damn," said the man in a soft, British accent.

Suleiman looked up as a young man entered carrying a Kalashnikov AK-47 assault rifle. The young man walked with a stick under one arm to support his weight since his left leg was gone at the knee. He held the rifle adeptly. He was short, but sturdy looking, with a voice that was steady, despite the message. "An Iraqi airplane is coming."

"Are you certain?" *Strange thought, Suleiman*, thought the Kurd.

"Yes. I can see the markings." He spit and looked at Suleiman's guest.

Suleiman also looked at his guest, then stood quickly

and took two metal hooks from beneath his bed. He went to the fire and drove the hooks into the soft dirt surrounding the blaze. With a quick jerk upwards, the fire lifted almost magically off the floor. He stood there for a moment holding a metal plate on which the fire burned. Then he nodded at the hole now replacing the fire, which seemed to disappear into blackness beneath the hut.

"Get inside and stay very quiet. If you're found, we'll all be executed," Suleiman ordered. The man did as he was instructed. Replacing the metal plate, Suleiman looked at the young man with the rifle. "Hide your weapon."

Reluctantly, the boy left the hut to hide his weapon.

Suleiman went outside where he saw the strange aircraft hovering over the village.

In the cockpit, Sacrette was scanning the faces of the villagers standing in the center of the small Kurdish village.

"Do you see him?" Farnsworth asked.

Sacrette was holding the aircraft in a hover while looking through binoculars. When he found one particular face in the crowd he smiled. "I'm going to set her down, right in the center of the village; pass the word. Nobody moves. I mean nobody!"

Suleiman watched as the Osprey with Iraqi markings slowly settled, whipping up a curtain of dust as the reversed props blasted against the ground. When the engines fell silent, he saw the side door open and a tall figure step through the settling cloud of swirling dust.

Sacrette was wearing the uniform of an Iraqi flight officer. His hands were clapped together, as though in prayer.

"He comes in peace," Suleiman said to himself. As Sacrette approached, he began to recall the swagger with which the pilot walked.

"Suleiman, my old friend." Sacrette approached wearing a broad grin.

Suleiman suddenly laughed, a belly laugh that turned his scowl to a smile. Stepping forward from the crowd, he embraced Sacrette. "Yes, it is you, my old friend. It has been many years since we first met."

"Many years." Sacrette smiled.

Suleiman examined the uniform, then looked at the Osprey. He knew the markings. "Have you left the American navy for the Iraqi air force?"

Sacrette shook his head. "No, old friend. I am here on a very delicate mission."

Suleiman thought for a moment. "The plane that looks like a bat and the pilot who is black?"

Sacrette felt a wave of relief. "I need to take them both back to my government."

Before Suleiman could reply, another voice interrupted, a British voice.

"You'll need the luck of the devil to pull that off, Captain Sacrette."

Sacrette looked past Suleiman to a man standing in the door of a hut.

A smile suddenly stretched across Sacrette's weathery features. "Well, I'll be a son of a bitch!"

The two men approached each other and embraced warmly.

Sacrette looked at the Brit. "Captain Jeremy Fallon, British intelligence. What in hell are you doing in this ancient part of the world?"

Fallon shook his head. A tuft of blond hair hung from

beneath the turban he wore. His green eyes sparkled. "I'm back with the SAS. I couldn't take the leisure life of being a spy."

Sacrette laughed. "You wouldn't be working for a Colonel Dillon, would you?"

Fallon showed surprise at hearing the name. "Dillon is my commanding officer. Where did you meet him?"

Sacrette explained. "But before we go to Kuwait, we have to recover the aircraft and the pilot."

A gloomy look filled Fallon's face.

"Problem?" asked Sacrette.

Fallon nodded. "The stealth is in the hills. It's in a cave and wired with explosives. The explosives can be neutralized easily enough. The pilot is another matter."

"What's happening?"

"There appears to be more players in the game than we realized." He looked at Suleiman. "A group of men were here. They claimed to be SAS, but they aren't. I have four teams working the area, these men were not part of my group. They have your pilot."

Sacrette started to understand. "That's why they're moving south."

"How do you know that?"

Sacrette explained the transmitter implanted in McGee's left armpit.

"In that case they should be easy enough to run down." He looked at the Osprey. "That is, if you're still as ballsy as you were in Nicaragua."

Nicaragua. Operation Sudden Fury. That was where Sacrette first met Fallon. Specifically, in the grimy jail in Ensenada, Mexico. Fallon had infiltrated a terrorist group en route to Nicaragua.

Sacrette looked at the Osprey. "This time I brought

along a few high-powered friends." He motioned to Farnsworth by pumping his arm up and down.

The SEALs piled out. They looked like a platoon of Iraqi soldiers.

Fallon took a small radio from inside his coat. He spoke quickly, ordering, "Bring them on in. The new arrivals are Americans."

Six minutes later five men appeared. They were as hearty looking as the SEALs. All were trained SAS dressed in the same clothes as Fallon, appearing to be Kurdish mountainmen.

Fallon introduced his SAS team, then suggested, "Let's take care of the stealth."

24

THE STEALTH WAS SITTING IN THE REAR OF A LARGE cave. Standing at the entrance, Sacrette was following the outline as Fallon held a high intensity flashlight on the fighter. The light paused at the opened bomb bay. A thin wire could be seen running from the bomb bay to the ground, where the wire disappeared.

"Watch your step, Boulton. The wire is a trip-wire." Fallon eased his way into the rich darkness of the cave, following the beam as though being towed by the light.

Once under the bomb bay, Fallon shone the light into the bay. Sacrette recognized the electronics pod. He also recognized something else. A package was taped to the pod.

"That looks like Czech Symtex," said Sacrette. He was looking at what appeared to be a one-kilo bundle of orange, plastic explosives. The package was wired for business.

"You're quite right."

"Commander." Sacrette raised his hand, motioning toward him.

Breaker LeDuc hurried to the stealth and knelt by the bay. After a quick, but careful perusal, his examination of the bundle was complete. "Piece of cake, captain." Carefully, he slipped inside the bay. Standing up, he put a small penlight in his mouth and removed a pair of wire cutters from a pouch on his webbing. A second later there was the sound of a snip, then another.

Still kneeling, Sacrette took a deep breath.

LeDuc knelt down. "All clear."

Sacrette looked around. "Check out the cockpit." Then he added, "Very carefully, commander."

Five minutes later LeDuc appeared at the entrance of the cave where Sacrette and Fallon were having a discussion. "The aircraft's secure. My men will remove the pod and put it in the Osprey. What do you want done with the stealth? Blow it up?"

Sacrette shook his head. "Not yet. We were ordered to bring the fighter back, if possible. First, we have to secure the pod, then find the pilot."

Back at the village, Sacrette and Fallon discussed the situation with Suleiman.

"Our orders are explicit, Boulton. We're to organize resistance in the event the balloon goes up in Desert Shield. I can't accompany you on the search for your pilot. But I can make certain the stealth is secure." There was an obvious look of disappointment on Fallon's face.

The same disappointment registered on the CAG's features.

"I understand, Jeremy. I can take the Red Cell team and get McGee." He looked at Suleiman, asking,

"You're certain there were only six other men with the pilot?"

Suleiman nodded. "The leader told me he was in the British army. I believed him. I believe anyone who says they need my help to kill Iraqis."

"What in the hell are they up to, Boulton?"

Sacrette shook his head. "I couldn't guess, except to say one thing: whatever it is, it's no good. Those bastards could start something with one shot."

Fallon grew curious at the thought. "You don't suppose . . . ?" His voice trailed off.

Sacrette released a long sigh at realizing the inference. "Christ. Are you thinking what I'm thinking?"

"Private interests," said Fallon.

"Yesterday morning, a Herky 130 filled with heavily-armed commando-types wearing freefall parachutes was shot down crossing into Syrian airspace. They weren't part of any operation mounted by our side and I doubt they were sent out of Iraq by the Iraqis. They were inbound to Iraq."

"To make a para drop."

"A para drop. An insert. But, why?"

"Private interests?"

"There you go, Jeremy. Private interests. The whole goddamned Gulf is sitting on the brink of what could be the first live-fire nuclear confrontation since World War II. The price of oil started to go through the roof until the diplomatic forces started to find some light in this dark tunnel, then oil prices started to go back down."

Fallon released a long whistle. "The price of oil would go to the stars if the oil fields in Iraq and Kuwait went up in flames. It doesn't matter what country is doing the selling, the price will still sky-rocket according to the law of supply and demand."

"Precisely. Cut back on the supply, and what does that do to the price on the demand side of the equation?"

"It makes a bloody ride in a lorry one expensive trip."

"Very expensive. Which brings us to two important questions: First, who are the players? Second, what are their intentions?"

Fallon mulled over the question. "The players are obviously not Arabs, at least not the men who have McGee. Brits. Perhaps other Europeans."

This was confirmed by Suleiman. "They were not Arab. They all spoke as though they were European."

"Mercenaries?" asked Sacrette.

"Probably. Question is: how many are there? Six mercs could do some damage, but more would be needed."

"The Herky. It carried forty-six. What if there were other groups air-dropped along the Iraqi border?"

"A bloody back-door operation. The Iraqis are watching the multi-national force in the desert and these buggers slip in and casually start the party."

"Exactly. There won't be any question-and-answer session. No diplomacy. Just tanks, troops, and aircraft kicking up a storm."

"And chemical weapons," Fallon added softly.

Suleiman's eyes widened. "Allah. What kind of men are these? They would destroy thousands—perhaps millions. Why?"

"Oil!" Sacrette and Fallon said in unison.

"They must be stopped," replied the old Kurd.

"Stopped? Quite right," said Fallon.

Sacrette offered the game plan. "Which means we have to know what they're planning. The group on the

Herky was a larger size force. The group holding McGee only has six men."

"What are you suggesting?" asked Fallon.

"The group holding McGee is the command post."

"Which means they'll be hooking up with other elements."

Sacrette nodded. "If not linking up, then certainly in communications." He looked at Suleiman. "Were the Europeans carrying radio equipment?"

Suleiman thought for a moment. "Yes. One carried a large radio on his back."

"A com base," said Fallon.

"That's the ticket. We have to take the command post. Then we'll get the information we need. Once we have the information, we have to take out the other groups. We've got the manpower. Your SAS team. My SEALs."

Fallon had a look that was incredulous. "You know what you're suggesting, Boulton?"

Sacrette nodded slowly. "We have to protect the Iraqis from being attacked."

Protecting a vicious, cruel enemy such as Iraq was the most painful thought the CAG had ever imagined.

25

1000.

THE SWEAT BURNED HIS EYES LIKE HOT, BOILING water. With his vision hazed, he could only walk one step at a time. His thought processes had ceased functioning an hour before. All he could do now was follow, rather, be led like a beast of burden, carrying the burden of his captors.

Major Sam McGee had been bound, hands behind his back, then tethered like a mule, with a rope around his neck. Adding to the insult, a heavy radio had been strapped to his back.

The six mercenaries had not stopped since the march began after McGee discovered they weren't British troops.

"Bloody kaffir," said the merc the others called Januf, a Pole who had spent eight years in the *Légion étrangére*, the French Foreign Legion, was a ruthless hulk of a man who had the original task of carrying the team's heavy radio. McGee now had that job and was doing poorly. "He looks spent."

Donaldson grumped, then laughed. "Have you seen a kaffir who could carry his weight?"

The others laughed, but kept moving through the harsh mountain range.

Kaffir! God how McGee hated that name. It was what the South Africans called the black Africans, people he could now empathize with, since he, too, was held in bondage.

But there was an important aspect of his existence that singled him out before the billions of people on the earth: a tiny pill-sized transmitter beaming a signal to a navsat somewhere above him.

Kaffir, indeed!

He was looking at the back of Donaldson's head.

His thoughts were private, his intentions colossal. *Your fucking balls are going to belong to me!* he vowed.

26

ADMIRAL LORD LEANED OVER THE SHOULDER OF THE exec, listening to the message coming from Sacrette. From his position, Sacrette had spoken into a communicator that cryptically encoded his message, then sent a one-hundredth-of-a-second laser burst to the satellite LaCrosse. The message was then transmitted from LaCrosse to the CIC in the *Valiant*.

Not a word had been intercepted. The message, if intercepted, would appear on receiving equipment as nothing more than a quick flash, like lightning, or a flaring sun spot.

Lord listened to the message: "Stealth in our control. Pod intact. Pilot in custody of unknown element. Element not Iraqi. Private interests. In pursuit."

Lord lifted a red telephone that immediately connected him to the chief of naval operations.

"We have an unexpected development," Lord reported, explaining the situation.

The voice of the CNO nearly ruptured Lord's eardrums.

"Captain Sacrette is keenly aware of the delicacy of the situation, admiral. I don't believe he would be taking action if it weren't critical." Lord was trying to explain, but again, as with the shooting down of the Hercules, he began to consider his retirement plans.

After the ass-chewing from the CNO, Lord went to his chair on the bridge. In the distance, the coast of Turkey was coming into view. Glaring at the loam-colored desert beyond the turquoise of the sea, he then looked to the south.

"My God," he breathed. "This could start World War III."

27

SACRETTE WAS SITTING IN THE COCKPIT OF THE OSprey studying the spot-check transmission from the LaCrosse. The spot check was being done every fifteen minutes to keep Sacrette in touch with McGee's position; the signature he was watching was from the locator worn by McGee. The area depicted on the digital display screen showed the Tigris and Euphrates. The signature had moved out of the Zagros mountains toward the Tigris.

"They're moving due west toward Mosul," said Sacrette.

"What do you suppose those buggers are up to?" asked Fallon.

Sacrette shook his head. His eyes slowly scanned the surrounding map key indicators. The indicators were simple enough: one indicated a city with a series of horizontal lines superimposed on a series of vertical lines.

An airstrip indicated a military airbase. A small rocket on a launcher indicated a SAM missile site. There was an airfield outside Mosul; adjacent to the airfield was a SAM missile site.

Fallon was sitting beside him, studying the map while sipping hot tea. He touched a particular indicator in the line of march of McGee's transmitter.

Sacrette turned to Fallon. "If you wanted to make a great deal of noise and get the biggest bang for your dollar, what would you do?"

Fallon answered without hesitation. "I suggest this is their target area."

Sacrette felt his skin crawl. "Christ. That would certainly make sense."

Fallon leaned into the screen. The indicator was cone-shaped. Next to the indicator symbol were three letters: NPP.

Sacrette gulped down the last of his hot tea. "A nuclear power plant."

"If I wanted to throw a spanner in the spokes, that would be my target."

"I have to agree. Tactically speaking, and politically, it's damned near perfect. I'd rule out the airbase. The base is too big a target for one team. The SAM site as well. But the power plant—they could start a world of shit with just the right amount of explosives."

"What's the number of European civilians in the complex?" asked Fallon.

"I have no idea. Intel has been scant at best."

Fallon shook his head. "The plant sits square on the banks of the Tigris. If the plant goes up, the contamination will run into the river to the Gulf, and only God knows where from there."

Sacrette checked his watch. "We leave in ten minutes. Get your people loaded."

"What do you have in mind?"

Sacrette pointed to the map. "The mercs appear to be following the track of this natural fissure in the earth's surface. It threads from the mountains toward the area northwest of the power plant." He tapped a village, then looked at Fallon. "Bring Suleiman."

Minutes later the old Kurd was in the cockpit of the Osprey. He appeared as out of place as Genghis Khan might have appeared standing in a submarine.

"Do you know Mosul?"

Suleiman's face brightened. "Many of my people live in Mosul."

"Do you know someone we can trust? Someone who will help?"

Suleiman shrugged. "No. We cannot trust any of them. Many Kurds have chosen the way of the Iraqis. Except those of us who have remained in Kurdistan."

"Which means we're on our own," Fallon pointed out.

Sacrette was studying McGee's locator transmission. "One thing is certain: we have to stop these characters. Getting there will be the task. We can't simply fly into the center of an Iraqi town in broad daylight, and without the Osprey we can't link up with LaCrosse to track McGee. Damn. We're shut off at every turn."

Fallon pointed out another shortfall in their composition. "There's the matter of our nationality to consider. We would never avoid detection. Strolling through the streets as tourists is definitely out."

Sacrette was trying to sort out all the liabilities. "More importantly, there's the matter of the pod and the stealth. That takes precedence. McGee is important, but he takes second cabin on this cruise."

Suleiman offered a suggestion. When finished, Fallon looked incredulously at Sacrette. "It might work. You can leave the SEALs here to guard the aircraft and the pod. We'll take the Red Cell team and my SAS team to Mosul."

Sacrette looked at Suleiman. "How far is Mosul?"

"Twenty-five kilometers."

Sacrette thought for a moment. "Fourteen miles." When his decision was made, he sent a laser-burst signal to Admiral Lord.

The message came in two parts, the second part sixty seconds behind the first.

Lord read the decoded crypto message. He looked at Opsta, then ordered, "Contact Desert Shield command in Saudi Arabia. Get everything on line. Captain Sacrette's going cross-country after McGee."

Lord felt confident the CAG could track McGee without the Osprey's tracking capabilities. At least, in theory, it should work.

The second part of the message was the most difficult to understand. Speaking to the commanding general of the Desert Shield operation, he told the army general, "There are unfriendly foreign elements inside Iraq. Their intentions are to obviously stir up an incident. I suggest we prepare for the worst."

28

1030.

THE EMERGENCE OF SADDAM HUSSEIN AND HIS ARAB Socialist Baath Party tore Iraq from the dusty, dingy swelter of being a Third World peasant state, to its present, modern position as one of the foremost, advanced, Arab countries. Oil had been the magic carpet that had brought the government to this point, then came war with Iran—a war fought over religious differences between the two nations. A war that killed nearly one million Arabs over an eight-year period. Iraqi and Iranian religious historians will claim the war was, indeed, fought over religion, but both sides knew that was just an excuse for the real reason: oil!

Khalid Ghani knew the truth. Lying next to Suad, the engineer ran his finger along the groove of her spine, she smelled of jasmine and incense. Her long hair covered her breasts. Her dark eyes were closed in sleep.

He tried to concentrate on her body, but his thoughts

kept drifting back to why he was in Mosul.

Khalid was an engineer. He was also Palestinian. Trained and educated in West Germany, he returned to Mosul, not for Suad, although it was certainly pleasurable being with her, but at the request of his commander, Ahmad Jibril, a former officer in the Syrian army, and leader of the Popular Front for the Liberation of Palestine—General Command (PELP-GC).

Khalid knew of the longstanding relationship between Latif and the man who had contracted Jibril and the Front: Ali Akhbar Murjan.

Khalid had personally built the detonator that became a trademark of Jibril's terror unit: a barometric device designed to detonate at a specific altitude, such as the one he built for Flight 103 that was destroyed over Lockerbie, Scotland.

Looking at a canvas bag on the floor, his white teeth gleamed from behind his moustache.

Then he felt Suad stroking his loins. "It is nearly time to leave," she said softly.

He checked his watch, then rolled her onto her stomach, whispering, "We have time. You don't leave for another hour."

In the kitchen below, Latif, too, was watching the time. Rising, he slipped through the back door and into the alley where he climbed into his car.

Speeding along, he drove out of Mosul, along the highway leading north. When he reached a curve in the road he turned onto a dirt road and drove east toward a natural landmark, a deep, natural fissure in the earth; a fissure running like a deep cut in the earth from the Zagros mountains.

29

1100.

CPO FARNSWORTH SAT ON THE FLOOR OF THE TRUCK staring glumly at the dark figures in front of him. The heat was nearly unbearable; the stench was even worse. He tried to rise but was shoved back to the floor by a large shape.

"Christ!" Farnsworth barked. "The bastard's standing on my foot."

Sacrette laughed. Looking past the tall, thin legs of the two huge camels standing over him, Farnsworth, too, started laughing while watching the CAG, the Red Cell team, and Fallon's SAS team. The men were all cramped in the rear of a lorry Farnsworth doubted could make it to Mosul.

The CPO summed up the situation simply: "I'm suffering heat exhaustion in Iraq, going further behind the enemy lines, and worst of all, I'm sitting hip deep in camel dung!"

Looming above the infiltrators were Suleiman's two prize camels, Hafez, the male, and Iftikar, the moon-eyed female.

"Camels are one of the most ancient forms of travel, Diamonds," said Fallon. "Long before horses, the Arabs rode camels. They are more suited for the climate than a horse, or a car, for that matter."

In the front of the lorry, Suleiman wasn't bothered by the stench; it was pure ambrosia to his nostrils. His camels were all he had in the world.

Noting a roadblock ahead, he stomped the floor several times.

"Quiet," ordered Sacrette.

Fallon stood and looked through a narrow slit in a canvas cover where the camels heads were protruding. When he saw the roadblock, he leaned down and whispered to one of his men. "Time to move, Connor."

An SAS soldier, a hulking Scot with red hair, slipped to the rear of the lorry. Reaching into his pack he removed a pistol, a scope was mounted on the black weapon. He inserted a slim, metal magazine, then perched himself on the rear gate of the lorry.

Suleiman eased to a stop in front of a pole blocking the road. A shack stood at the roadside. An Iraqi soldier was standing by the pole while another was walking from the shack toward the lorry.

"Steady, lads," Fallon cautioned the men. All fingers were on the triggers of their weapons. All weapons were switched off safety.

A soldier approached, holding out his hand to Suleiman. The Kurd handed the soldier his internal travel documents. The soldier went to the guard shack and checked the papers against a list of wanted criminals.

The second soldier stepped suspiciously around the lorry, examining first the undercarriage, then the siding. Looking up, he noticed the head of a camel.

He laughed at the sight, then continued around to the rear where the canvas hung over a box frame mounted on the bed of the lorry.

Sitting on the gate, the Scot held the pistol at the ready. His breathing was suppressed to the point of barely breathing at all. Trained for close-in work, he had long ago learned how to reduce his pulse and respiration to a minimal rate. A stream of sweat was different, however, a stream that ran into his eyes, triggering the instinctive need to wipe.

He held concrete still. He could hear the soldier beyond the canvas curtain.

In the darkness beneath the canvas, Fallon slowly raised his weapon.

That was when providence intervened.

Hafez, the male camel, expelled a long rush of wind as his bowels emptied.

The smell was nearly overwhelming for the Scot, but it served to save the moment.

Smelling the miasma, the Iraqi soldier cursed, then walked back to the guard post and waved the "all clear" signal to the other guard.

Suleiman shifted gears, and the lorry passed slowly through the checkpoint.

In the rear, the Scot lowered himself to the floor of the flatbed.

A trickle of laughter filtered through the darkness, laughter that erupted into a howling din for all but one.

On the floor, Diamonds sat wiping fresh camel shit off the top of his head.

30

Desert Shield Command, Saudi Arabia.

THE SITUATION WAS BECOMING WORSE BY THE DAY for the Commanding General of Operation Desert Shield. For months, elite troops had sat in the sand, dug in for an assault that, if it did come, could produce more casualties in one day than in the entire Vietnam war.

Tanks were not proving out in the desert, helicopters were becoming sand clogged, filters that were supposed to do the job were not adequate. The heat was worse than the Mojave. Crack fighting troops, the elite of the elite, were sitting on their asses doing what they weren't trained to do: wait for an enemy.

Worst of all was the human toll: dozens of men had been killed, multi-million-dollar airplanes lost.

The Rapid Deployment Force (RDF) was a mobile, quick-hit, knock-out punch that was standing in the desert with its dick in its hand.

The initiative had been lost. Now, so had a stealth

fighter and its pilot. And Americans inside Iraq had encountered a plot to heat up the theater of operation.

Reaching for the red telephone sitting on a communications system unequaled except for the U.S. president's, the CG inserted a computer card into a slot and waited for the cryptic telephone number to ring on the other side of the world.

A few seconds later the voice of the president came on the line. He sounded half asleep.

"My apologies, Mr. President. We have a situation that requires your immediate attention."

The CG explained.

"Recall them, dammit."

"That's impossible, Mr. President. They are out of radio contact."

"Who authorized this operation, general?"

There was a pause. "You did, sir. You approved the 'black operation' to extract the pilot and recover the stealth. This is a residual effect of the operation. It happens. Men of Captain Sacrette's training are expected to take the initiative if there is no time for approval. Apparently, this is one of those situations."

There was a long pause from the other end, then, without a word, the president hung up and lay back on his pillow. He thought for a long, agonizing moment.

Finally, he dialed one of his closest advisors. After apologizing for the lateness of the hour, he explained the situation.

The president listened to the advice. He didn't like what he heard.

"Mr. President, I suggest we establish a back-channel to the Baghdad government. That will insure the Iraqi government doesn't do anything rash."

The president thought for a moment. "My God. Do you know what you're suggesting?"

"Yes, sir. The elements will no doubt be captured by the Iraqis. We give up a pawn to save the king."

The president thought for a moment. His mind was racing with the possibilities, all potentially disastrous. "Will the Iraqis go for a deal like that? What if they suspect it's a trick?"

"Why should they, Mr. President? We're the ones losing our men to save them from being forced into a war they can't win. We're the ones with egg on our face."

"What about the political fall-out?"

"That's part of the deal. The United States and Iraq will officially go on record with the Secretary General of the United Nations. We're covered if Hussein tries to make a political debacle out of the incursion. It's a humanitarian mission."

"What about our men? How do we explain their original presence?"

"That's part of any war, Mr. President. The public will have expected you to do something to give us the edge in case of war. As far as our men are concerned—that's part of the deal—nothing happens to our people. The Iraqis pick them up and return them to our forces. In exchange, we cooperate to track down the people inside Iraq. That can't be done without our cooperation."

"How do we explain this to the American people?"

His advisor chuckled. "We don't."

"You mean—it never happened?"

"That's correct, Mr. President. It never happened."

31

1315.

McGee was pulled roughly from the trunk of the car he had been riding in for nearly an hour. He was soaked with sweat and thought he would die from the heat. He was blindfolded and his head covered with a hood from a heavy robe, making the heat that much more intolerable.

Beside the pungent odor of stale booze, he could smell the odor of food as he was led into the rear of what he thought was a café, or possibly a bar.

The voices he heard were speaking Arabic; all except one belonged to an Arab. One of the voices was apparently giving the Brit, Donaldson, bloody hell.

"You must be insane for bringing him with you," Khalid shouted.

"He'll be valuable, so settle your feathers and find me a place to stash this bloke. We have much to do before we get on to Baghdad." There was a pause, then Donaldson asked, "Has the woman left for Baghdad? My people will be expecting her at the rendezvous."

Khalid nodded reassuringly. "She is already on the way."

Donaldson was talking now as he removed the hood and blindfold from McGee.

When McGee could finally see, he was sitting in the rear of what he knew was a restaurant. An old man seemed to be in control, and a younger man with fiery eyes staring at him with loathing.

It was at that moment he knew his life was on very thin ice.

Khalid threw his head at McGee. "What do you plan to do with him?"

Donaldson laughed. He reached to McGee's uniform and pulled at the fighter group patch sewn on his sleeve. "What better way to make Hussein believe the nuclear plant was blown up by Americans than to have the Iraqi police find an American pilot—a stealth pilot—hiding in the city?"

Khalid thought about the notion for a moment. He looked at Latif, who nodded approvingly. "Perhaps it is a good plan."

Donaldson bowed arrogantly. "Delighted you approve. Now, where are your bona fides?"

Khalid went up the stairs and returned carrying a heavy suitcase.

"Get him upstairs," Khalid insisted as he looked at McGee.

McGee was dragged upstairs and laid on a bed. His hands were freed by Donaldson, who reminded the pilot, "I wouldn't try to escape. You wouldn't get ten feet in this city wearing that American flight suit."

The merc laughed throatily and left the room.

Latif was pouring tea when Donaldson returned. The suitcase was open, lying on the table. Khalid was holding a long, cylindrical device.

"Is that it?" asked Donaldson.

Khalid handed the explosive device to the mercenary. "It doesn't look big enough to be effective," said the Brit.

Khalid laughed. "It has more than enough explosive force. All that is needed is to create an explosion in the reactor. The chain reaction that will follow will do the rest."

Latif interrupted. "What about the rest of your men? Are they in position?" he asked Donaldson.

Donaldson checked his watch. "All but one group. One group has not reported in."

Latif didn't look surprised. "They won't be reporting. I was informed last night one of your group was destroyed entering Syrian airspace."

"Damn," Donaldson spit. "That was the group assigned to the oil fields and chemical plant near Kirkuk."

Latif was a man who had known disappointment too often to be disturbed by the loss of one element. It was the overall plan that mattered. "The other groups are in Baghdad. They will be contacted by my representative. The mission will still be a success."

Donaldson grumped. "You bloody well better hope so, Latif. Otherwise, Ali Akhbar Murjan will have our heads on a pole."

Latif smiled; he was an old man who no longer feared death. He checked his watch. "You and your men will remain upstairs. You will be transported to Baghdad this afternoon."

There was a long pause, then Khalid spoke. "Do you have the detonator?" he asked Donaldson.

Donaldson smiled. When approached to join Murjan, Donaldson had credentials few other mercenaries in the world would have. A former SAS soldier, he had once been assigned to the British nuclear weapons program as a security specialist. While serving in that capacity he made friends with a scientist who had a penchant for young boys. Donaldson kept that information, and certain photographs, to himself, never knowing they would be valuable. Through the grapevine he was contacted by Murjan, who had a specific request, a request he could fulfill only by approaching the homosexual scientist.

Fearing exposure, the scientist did as Donaldson instructed.

Donaldson reached into his pocket and removed a small, metallic disc. Handing the disc to Khalid, he said, "Compliments of a highly-paid scientist on Her Majesty's nuclear arms project."

Khalid's eyes widened. Quickly, he reached for the suitcase and removed the explosive device. Taking the detonator, he carefully inserted the disc into a round opening, checking for fit. "Perfect."

They all stared at the device. Moments before it was a rather harmless looking contraption.

Now, with the detonator in place, the device was a miniature nuclear weapon!

32

1355.

In the stealth hangar at Al Salamiyah airbase, Aaron Feinberg had his nose pressed against a computer projecting a detailed map display of Mosul. He was tired, the fatigue showing on his face; coffee jitters had started earlier that morning and he was now approaching the point of near collapse.

The signature from McGee's transmitter was now stationary, suggesting the pilot was no longer on the move.

"They've either put him in cold storage," Feinberg whispered, "or they've cut his throat and left him in an alley." Either way, Feinberg knew it was time to move.

Sacrette and the SEALs had been out of satellite communications since leaving the Osprey. Before departing Ishtar, the CAG had sent instructions, instructions Feinberg hoped would work. Glancing over his shoulder, he looked at a young airwoman sitting at a mobile radio station.

"Get ready, miss. You're about to go on the air."

The airwoman adjusted her headset and turned several dials on the transmitter sitting in front of her.

Watching the seconds tick off on his watch, Feinberg raised his hand. When the time went straight up to 1400, Feinberg flashed his finger at the airwoman.

She leaned into the microphone, and with a voice sweet as honey, said softly . . .

"Good afternoon, Saudi Arabia. This is Armed Forces Radio!"

33

SACRETTE SAT IN THE FRONT OF THE LORRY WITH Suleiman. In his lap he held a transistor radio purchased by Suleiman from a shop on the bazaar shortly after entering Mosul. A wire ran from the radio, which was tuned into the AFR frequency, to Sacrette's ear. On his lap was a detailed map of the city belonging to Fallon.

When the soft voice of the AFR deejay began talking, he knew the message would not be meant for him until the deejay reached that part of the program the troops in the desert listened to religiously—Messages from Home.

Messages from Home had been a daily part of the Vietnam soldiers routine, listening for that one moment when they might hear a special song played from a loved one, or a message called in by telephone from the United States.

In Desert Shield, the AFR went on the air, playing

music, giving world news and sports, like any other radio station. The radio also served another keen function discovered in Vietnam:

It was a superb form of directing covert operations in the field without breaking radio silence, or if there was no possible radio contact, which was Sacrette's case.

"This message is for Captain Boulton Sacrette aboard the carrier U.S.S. *Valiant.* Your package arrived safely. Thank you, dear. As you know, our son's birthday is coming up and I know he'll love the gifts. Eddie will be four years old on the sixth. It's too bad you won't be here to celebrate at the party. Oh, well, next year. In the meantime, we love you and miss you. Good-bye, dear."

Sacrette looked at the map resting on his knee. Like most maps, it was layed out in alphanumeric grids.

Quickly he deciphered the code.

Eddie. Section E.

Four years old. Section 4.

E-4.

Running down the map, he intersected E and 4.

"Do you know this area?" Sacrette asked Suleiman.

Suleiman studied the street name. "Yes. It is a very bad part of the city filled with thieves, murderers, prostitutes. Very bad."

Sacrette smiled. "Perfect. We won't look too out of place." He nodded. "Let's go."

As the lorry pulled away, Sacrette leaned through a flap separating the cab from the bed.

"Hang on, gentlemen. We have McGee's location and are en route."

The lorry rumbled along the highway outside Mosul, with the two camels' heads jutting up, looking curiously around as they entered the city.

In the back of the lorry, the men were nearly spent from the heat, the cramped conditions and, worst of all, the stench from the camels.

They could have cared less what awaited them. What they wanted was out!

If that meant dying or killing it didn't matter.

Killing would be a gift from God.

Dying meant nothing—they already felt dead!

34

1600.

ON A MAP, LATIF'S OLD FINGERS DREW A SLOW, ALmost painful trail along the ridges of an area northwest of Mosul. The map was spread on a table, drawing the attention of the mercenaries. Donaldson and his men were standing around the table, studying the areas specifically marked by three red circles.

One was the nuclear power plant. The second was an oil pipeline. The third was an Iraqi petroleum pumping station.

Donaldson did the talking, explaining to his men their individual assignments.

"We'll operate in two three-man teams. Standard SAS tactics." He looked at Dugan, the surly, flat-faced Scotsman. "Dugan's team will blow up the oil depot northwest of the city. The nuclear power plant is scheduled to go at midnight. The oilfield has to go at 2356. That will make it appear that an air attack came from across the Turkish border."

He looked at Januf, the Polish mercenary, and Kurt, the German. "Januf and Kurt will go with me to the pumping station." He tapped a point on the map a few miles from Mosul; the pumping station was across the Tigris. He looked severely at Latif. "You're certain you can get us across the bridge."

The old man nodded confidently.

"Good. We'll blow up the pumping station at precisely 2357." He glanced around. "Any questions?"

There were none. "Good. Get some rest. We have a long night."

The men went upstairs where rooms had been arranged for them. Latif poured tea for himself and Donaldson. Sitting down, the old man wanted to cover one last point.

"What about the American pilot?"

Donaldson leered. "I'll let you take care of the American. He can be useful covering our tracks. Shoot him. Cut his throat. I don't care. I want his aircraft. At least the electronics aboard. I know people in South Africa who will pay a fortune for the equipment aboard the fighter."

There was a devious look in Latif's eyes. "I know a more useful means of disposing of the pilot."

"What?"

"My people in Beirut. The Hazbollah."

"I thought your government was softening its mood toward the Americans, trading the hostages in Beirut and all that rot for renewing diplomatic relations?"

Latif's features never flinched. "A wise man never sells

all his grain. The winter to come may be worse than anticipated."

Donaldson laughed. "The game goes on, eh, mate?"

The old man shrugged innocently. "We do what we must do, *fendi*."

Donaldson took a metallic flask from his coat. He poured a shot of scotch whiskey into his cup. "This has turned out better than I had imagined, old man. It'll be a profitable venture on my part. Profitable indeed."

The old man looked at the flask, then at the man. There was the look of the devil in his eyes.

More so than you might think, thought Latif. *More so than you might think*.

35

ADMIRAL LORD WAS SO SHAKEN BY WHAT HE'D HEARD he stormed from the CIC without a word. He went straight for his seacabin off the bridge and opened a liquor cabinet beneath his desk. Taking a bottle of Glenfarclas Scotch whiskey, he poured a healthy glass of the 104 proof, aged Scotch and tossed down the booze like it was Kool Aid.

He sat thinking for a long moment. Memories flashed through his mind, memories covering over two decades as a naval midshipman, aviator, CAG, and finally, admiral of a carrier battle group.

"Those bastards!" He roared, rising to look at the bottle. He took a long, healthy swig, felt his stomach burn, then clamped the bottle soundly onto the desk next to his typewriter.

An hour later, Admiral Lord had finished half the bottle of Scotch and all of the letter he was writing.

He walked numbly from his seacabin to the commo center where he found a young ensign. He handed the hastily written page to the ensign, then barked, "FAX this letter to the chairman of the Joint Chiefs. ASAP!"

Lord started through the door. The ensign had already read the two-paragraph statement and called to the admiral, "Are you certain of this, sir?"

Lord turned on the young man with eyes that could melt steel. "Send it, damn you. Now!"

Thirty minutes later, the word had spread throughout the *Valiant*: The admiral had resigned from the navy!

36

Baghdad, Military Command Headquarters.

GENERAL YOUSOF NAJAF LOOKED UP FROM HIS DESK as an excited young captain entered his office. Yousof, a heavyset man with long, porkchop sideburns, was one of the few generals to survive the years since Saddam Hussein took command of the government. He remembered the night in the Abbasid Palace when Hussein walked down the "long line of death"—twenty-two officers were on their knees, their hands bound, their mouths gagged.

Beside Hussein walked Najaf, holding his pistols.

One by one, the officers were shot in the head by Hussein. When a pistol emptied, he extended his hand to Najaf and continued along the line of condemned officers.

A similar incident occurred the night the Iraqis invaded Kuwait. On that night over 120 officers were executed for refusing to obey Hussein's orders to invade.

Najaf knew better than to cross Hussein, unless there was no doubt the madman could be stopped.

And stopped he had to be, which was why Najaf was receptive to overtures from a cartel sheik, through a middleman, of course, suggesting Najaf would be the next leader of Iraq—a very wealthy next leader—if he cooperated.

He cooperated. Not for the money in the Swiss bank account deposited by the cartel. Not for the power.

But for Iraq.

Or so he made himself believe, which was why he had selected a certain intelligence officer, Colonel Abu Az Ahmedsa.

May the fleas of a thousand camels infest the crotches of his children, he cursed, as he read the communique handed him by the captain.

"Have you read this, captain?" he asked sharply.

"Of course. I received the message myself not ten minutes ago."

"Has the message been relayed to the president?"

The captain smiled. "No, sir. I knew you would want to personally take the message to the president."

Najaf smiled appreciatively. "You have a great future ahead, captain. But tell me, has the message been received by any other government agency? This is important. I wouldn't want to arrive after some *shamoot* from the diplomatic corp had delivered the message ahead of me."

The captain grinned. "No, sir. The message was sent from the Secretary General at the United Nations. Apparently, the secretary is trying to keep this information on an 'eyes only' basis."

Najaf nodded. "You may return to your duties."

The captain started toward the door. He didn't notice Najaf's hand move quickly to the drawer in his desk.

Reaching the door, his hand about to grasp the handle, he turned as he heard Najaf say, "There is one more thing, captain."

The captain turned, and grew wild-eyed as he stared at the muzzle of a small pistol.

The weapon barked once. The bullet found its mark in the captain's throat.

Moving swiftly, Najaf took the body to his coat closet. Hanging the dead man on a hook, he went and checked for blood.

A crimson splotch on the marble floor was easily wiped up.

Two minutes later Najaf was in his car, driving furiously along Haifa Street. He crossed the Tigris at the Jumhuriyah Bridge, then turned on Sadun Street. He wasn't certain what lay ahead, but he knew what lay behind.

He couldn't go back!

His staff car rolled to a screech at the Baghdad Hotel.

He took the elevator to the tenth floor where he knocked impatiently on the door and waited nervously.

When the door opened he saw a beautiful, long-haired woman standing framed in the soft light bleeding from the room.

"Come in, general." Suad Samarallah motioned for the general to enter the room.

What he found waiting was not only unsettling, but reaffirmed his previous notion that he had passed the point of no return.

Standing in the room, their weapons drawn, were four

men. They weren't "guests" as hostages in the other hotels had become.

A tall man approached. His accent was British—Cockney. " 'Ave a chair, general." He pointed at several bottles on the dresser. "Care to have a drink?"

Najaf shook his head. "This is not the time to drink. The United Nations knows about your plan."

The Brit took a bottle of Johnny Walker Red and poured a large drink. He thought for a moment. "How do you know?"

"The message came less than thirty minutes ago."

"Who else saw the message?"

He shrugged. "No one but myself, but there will be other messages. I had to kill the officer who received the message. We must get out of Baghdad. Now!"

The Cockney, who was known only as "Jocko," took a long, languid drink. Appearing to have made a decision, he turned back to Najaf. "That's impossible. Our explosives are already in place. There is nothing to do but push forward. We wait for the signal from Donaldson. When the signal comes, we punch the button."

"How will you know?"

Jocko laughed. "When the nuclear power plant at Mosul goes up, electricity will be cut off throughout the city. Every aircraft in the Iraqi air force will be off the ground. Don't worry, mate. We'll know. A whole shit storm will come raining down on this pisshole of a country. Then we'll drive Mr. Hussein absolutely mad from our end. When we're finished he'll start war with your precious Allah."

Jocko went to a window and stepped out onto the balcony. In the distance, the first traces of darkness were starting to sweep in from the east. His keen eyes studied a peculiar shape rising above the capital.

East, near Saddam City, a tall, black structure loomed above the mystical city. Shaped like an upside down top divided into two sections, the Monument of Saddam Hussein's Qadissya Martyr's honored the 70,000 Iraqis killed in the war with Iran.

"President Hussein will bloody well shit when that monstrosity comes tumbling down." He playfully pointed an electronic detonator at the monument and whispered, "Pow!"

Najaf's voice became a near shriek. "You're insane. The city will be closed off within an hour. We have to get out of Baghdad. Now."

Jocko checked his watch. "We have five hours. Who cares that Hussein knows? The explosives are in place. Once the explosives have been detonated, we're skating in the clear. Our money is in the bank. I won't let you ruin that, general. Besides, you said the message was sent to you. If another message arrives, your subordinates won't do anything without contacting you first."

Jocko nodded to the figure that had slipped behind the general.

Najaf started to protest, but was suddenly stung by a sharp pain in his back.

He looked around, panicked, and saw Suad standing behind him. Her hand was gripping the handle of a dagger.

The dagger had pierced Najaf's kidney.

Najaf started to scream, but Jocko moved swiftly, clamping his hand over the dying general's mouth.

The tall Cockney held the man, who was in the final shudders of his death throes.

His last vision was Jocko's sneering face.

37

1700.

Darkness was falling over Mosul as Sacrette peered through a pair of binoculars. He had studied the various buildings on the street, but only one appeared suspicious.

"There's no traffic coming or going from the restaurant in the middle of the street."

Suleiman pointed at the front door. A sign in Arabic read: CLOSED. "I know this restaurant. It is very popular. The owner never closes, not even on religious holidays."

Sacrette turned to Fallon, who was peering through the slot. "What do you think?"

"I think we better have a closer look."

Sacrette instructed Suleiman to drive around the block. Turning left at the end of the street, they noticed an alley threading through the center of the block. Sacrette motioned Suleiman to continue. On the opposing side of the block there was a burned-out building nearly directly behind the restaurant.

"Let's use the building for an observation post," suggested Fallon.

It was dark now, the darkness providing perfect cover for the American and Brit commandos. Silently, they slipped into the burned-out remnants of a two-story building.

Fallon sent one man topside, and LeDuc sent Lipp with the Brit. In position, they scanned the back of the restaurant.

"I've got movement in the top room, mate," whispered the Brit.

Lipp studied the room at the top of the restaurant. A man was walking around inside. He appeared to be pacing.

Lipp motioned with his head. "Get Sacrette and Fallon."

Minutes later, the two commanders were studying the figure in the window.

Suddenly, Fallon stiffened. "Bloody hell!"

"Do you recognize him?"

Fallon's teeth gritted. "Former—and I do mean former—Captain Norwood Cullen Donaldson. Ex-para, formerly of the SAS. He was thrown out two years ago. Word around the service is he's gone private. Mercenary."

"That fits the bill. We've found the command post."

"What now?"

Sacrette looked menacingly at Fallon. "Time to trip the lights fantastic!"

38

SECURITY HAD BEEN ABANDONED. THE COMMUNICATION between Admiral Lord and the Seal Two team leader was transmitting in the clear. "Can you fly the Osprey?" asked Lord. He was sitting in his seacabin, patched through to Commander Davies by satellite link-up.

"Yes, sir." A strained pause followed. "Do you think that's necessary?"

"Damned necessary. The State Department has contacted the Iraqis, informing them of the infiltrators. That leaves Captain Sacrette and his men with their butts hanging out. I want that pod brought out."

"Christ Almighty. Whose damned fine idea was it to inform the Iraqis?"

"The high command, which means the situation will have already started to become fluid. Get your people aboard the Osprey and return to the *Valiant*."

"Isn't there something we can do for Captain Sacrette and our people?"

Lord shook his head sadly. "We can only hope the Iraqis show some compassion. If Captain Sacrette's picked up, he could be treated as a spy, regardless of the agreement between our two governments."

"That won't be the case, sir. Captain Sacrette won't know about the agreement. If he sees an Iraqi soldier, he'll start shooting. I would."

Lord didn't respond to the comment. Instead, he snapped, "Get your people and the pod aboard the Osprey and return to the carrier. Is that understood?"

"Yes, sir." The connection went dead from the village in Iraq.

39

1730.

FROM OPPOSING ENDS OF THE ALLEY, THE SAS AND Red Cell Four teams moved with feline grace, staying tight against the shadows. Their feet barely touched the ground; their footsteps were silent. All of their equipment was tied down; the safeties on their weapons filed nearly flush, providing only an ounce of friction against the trigger. An ounce that would hold the weapon on safe, yet could be easily pulled through if necessary to fire without notice.

Nearing the rear of the restaurant, Brooks Bollinger gripped a drainpipe running from the roof. Without hesitation the demo expert scaled the pipe until he was beneath the window overlooking the alley. From inside he could hear the sound of voices speaking in English. Looking down, he nodded at LeDuc.

Fallon stood on one side of the rear door with his SAS team; Sacrette was at his side. On the other side of the door LeDuc carefully turned the handle.

Locked!

LeDuc gritted his teeth and pointed at Lipp. The young SEAL took a leather pouch from his pocket. Removing a lock pick, he carefully slid the pick into the lock. Seconds later, he felt the tumbler slide.

Nodding at Sacrette, LeDuc took in a deep breath as he pulled a 9mm automatic from inside his coat.

Latif heard nothing. Reading the Koran, as he did daily, he was reaching for a cup of tea when he felt the hair on his neck prickle. His head turned, and seeing the door crack slightly, he started to rise.

LeDuc fired. The bullet made no noise, except the sickening cough as the projectile entered the old man's head at the base of the skull. His head jerked wildly, his arms flew straight out, then his body pitched forward.

Still seated, the disciple of Khomeini lay face down on the Koran, his blood soaking into the pages.

At that moment the door opened and the commandos entered in silence.

Fallon was at the lead, with the others following. Quickly, he moved to the stairs and was starting up with his Uzi aimed toward the top, when he heard a voice and withdrew back down the stairs.

The mercenary descending the stairs was dressed in nothing but his shorts. Slung from his shoulder was an AK-47, which dangled loosely at his side. Reaching the last step, he saw the old man and started to shout when LeDuc's hand clamped onto his mouth.

With lightning speed, Fallon grasped the merc's hands while Lipp, a former wrestler, shot for his legs. Lipp hoisted the merc off his feet, and with his hands captured by Fallon, it took only the move of LeDuc's free hand to send the mercenary to oblivion.

LeDuc thrust his commando knife savagely, but accurately, at the merc's throat. Supporting the dying man's weight, Lipp could feel the blood running from the man's throat onto his chest, then pooling over his stomach before the sticky gore oozed onto the young SEAL's shoulder.

The commando's knew it took time for a man to die from a knife wound. With the carotid artery severed, life drains quickly, but a knife kill, like a garrote, required patience. The men held the merc's body in silence as he jerked spasmodically, still trying to resist.

Finally, there was a shudder, and the release of the sphincter, and they knew the merc was dispatched.

Reaching into his pocket, Fallon removed a tiny capsule and motioned to the others. LeDuc and Lipp took a similar capsule from their pockets. Each man popped the capsules in their mouths and crunched down.

"Come along, lads," Fallon whispered. LeDuc and Lipp followed the Brit up the stairs.

Reaching the top of the stairs, Fallon checked his watch. He held up his hand. Five fingers extended as he began the countdown.

Four fingers. He hoisted his Uzi, the silencer pointed at the top of the steps.

Three. He moved the safety switch.

Two. He started up, then—

One!

From outside the window, Bollinger released the spoon on a stun grenade and shoved the device through the window.

A loud explosion followed. The room turned white-hot with the brilliant glare as the grenade, designed to momentarily paralyze the optic nerves, turned the five mercenaries into statues.

The only ones safe from the effects were the men coming through the door; men who moments before had taken a chemical agent that would retard the paralyzing effect of the gas.

Donaldson was facing the door when he saw one of those men enter, a man he recognized from Sandhurst and his days in the SAS.

Jeremy Fallon said nothing. Leering demonically, he stepped forward and slammed the butt of his Uzi against the merc's jaw.

Donaldson pitched over, unable to move. He could still hear, and recognized the muted sound of the automatics as the intruders swept the room with accurate, deadly gunfire.

It was over in three seconds.

One merc was cleaning his weapon when the grenade exploded. He looked up, frozen by the chemical, and could only stare at the burly LeDuc pulling the trigger of his MAC-10. The bullets stitched five clean holes through his chest and throat.

Another merc found neither mercy, nor pity, from Lipp, who fired one six-round burst from his MAC-10. The merc flew backward from where he sat on the floor, finally stopping against the wall.

The last merc died equally as fast, in a hailstorm of punishing bullets from Bollinger, who leaned through the window and released a long tongue of withering firepower.

"All clear," shouted Fallon, who moved quickly to where Donaldson lay in a heap on the floor. Flipping the mercenary on his side, he quickly bound and gagged the man with whom he once served in the Falklands.

"Who dares—Wins! Cullen, my boy. You should have stayed in London."

Donaldson's garbled voice was less than a whimper as he was jerked to his feet.

"Where's the American pilot?" Fallon demanded.

Donaldson nodded weakly at a curtain. Pulling back the curtain, Fallon smiled at the man sitting on the floor. His hands were tied, and there was a glaze in his eyes, but he was alive.

"Major McGee, I presume."

Major Sam McGee pulled himself to his feet. He was grinning from ear to ear.

Fallon untied his hands. "An old friend of yours is waiting downstairs."

"BLOODY BASTARD," FALLON BREATHED HEAVILY. HE was watching Donaldson sit rather casually in the chair occupied minutes before by the dead Latif. Whispering to Sacrette, he said, "We don't have much time, captain. This bloke's a real hardcase. He could hold out all night if necessary."

"We may not have all night. You heard McGee—one of them has a nuclear device. He's probably already at the nuclear plant."

LeDuc stepped beside Sacrette. "Give me a few minutes alone with him, captain. All I need is a cigarette lighter and a pair of pliers. I'll strip the skin off this smartass."

Sacrette spoke aloud, wanting the mercenary to hear his idea. "I've got a better plan. We'll tie him up and leave him here, then call the Iraqi police. I'm sure their methods of persuasion are much more effective."

This notion immediately caught Donaldson's attention. "You wouldn't. Besides, I know where the stealth is located. Not to mention Fallon—I'm certain his team isn't the only SAS team inside Iraq." His voice had an air of arrogance.

Diamonds leaned to Sacrette. "He's got us by the short hairs, captain. Why don't we just slit his throat and get the hell out of Dodge?"

Sacrette dismissed the advice by pointing out the obvious. "There's a crazy man with a nuclear device about to get a lot of people killed. A lot of those people will be American troops. We can't pull out until this matter is settled."

Fallon checked his watch. "Then it's time to bargain with the devil."

Sacrette's mouth tightened. "Christ. I'd like to shove his teeth down his throat."

Fallon pushed his point again. "Time, captain. We're running out of time."

Sacrette was fit to be tied, but he knew Fallon was right. Time was running out. Whatever Donaldson knew—it would take a deal to extract. Looking at Fallon, Sacrette hissed, "Make a deal."

Baghdad.
1830.

JOCKO SAT ON THE EDGE OF THE BALCONY OVERlooking the Baghdad Hotel, watching the swimming pool below. The mood lights in the water turned the pool a soft red, giving it the look of blood. Suad was sitting on the bed reading the Koran. The others were watching the television, where an old "Mr. Ed" show was playing.

Taking a bottle of Scotch, Jocko poured a drink, then gulped down the whiskey. In his pocket was the remote detonator, which he tapped occasionally as though reminding himself it was still on his person.

His thoughts drifted to the bank account he would soon enjoy. The money, the women he could afford. No more fighting in backwater countries for low-life dictators. No more risking his life for pennies.

He would be set.

That was when the door exploded open.

Four soldiers dressed in fatigues stepped through the door, their AK-47s blazing.

On the bed, Suad was shredded by a dozen bullets that tore her upper torso completely in half. The men watching "Mr. Ed" never saw the ending. They were killed instantly.

On the balcony, Jocko took a full blast of bullets in the chest. He was lifted off the balcony and thrown into the empty air above the pool.

Falling end over end, he tried to grab the detonator but felt nothing but the gore where his chest had been.

"Donaldson!" he screamed, but the name came out as nothing more than a whisper.

Down he fell, striking the edge of the pool before his body rolled into the water.

The soft red of the water now turned a deep crimson where the mercenary's blood drained into the pool.

42

The nuclear power plant outside Mosul sat in a sea of bright lights; protected by a high security fence, armed soldiers and guard dogs, entrance was difficult at best, damned near impossible at worst. In the distance, an Iraqi airbase and a SAM missile site offered further deterrence to an air attack.

Khalid Ghani didn't fear the obstacles. He drove into the parking lot behind the wheel of a van marked Kassim's Catering Service. Glancing at the front entrance, he could see a long line formed by plant personnel snaking from the first of many security checkpoints. He passed through the parking lot to a small road that wound toward another gate marked in Arabic: DELIVERIES.

Nearing the gate, he reached into his pocket and removed a plastic identification badge bearing his photograph.

He had no more than pinned the badge to the white

servant jacket he was wearing when he heard the ear-piercing wail of a siren.

Suddenly, troop carriers began appearing. Soviet-made BMP's roared through the parking lot, the turrets of the armored personnel carriers manned by soldiers behind heavy machine guns.

The air filled with the flutter of rotor slap. Bright flood-lights burned from the noses of the helicopters searching the area.

That's when a cold chill streaked along his spine and he knew they we were looking for him!

In seconds, the van was suddenly surrounded by BMP's, jeeps, troops on foot, and hovering heloes.

That was when he heard a metallic voice issue an order from a loudspeaker mounted on one of the hovering helicopters. "Khalid Ghani. You are surrounded. Put up your hands and get out of the van."

The voice of the Iraqi soldier issued the order a second time. Khalid glanced at the briefcase on the floor. The timer was preset.

With the ferocity of a madman, Khalid reached for the briefcase. Framed in the light, the soldiers saw his movement. Khalid opened the top of the briefcase and reached inside to where the computerized timing-device had one particular wire that would at least give him some satisfaction of victory.

Finding a blue wire, the booby-trap wire, he started to pull it free to detonate the device.

That was when the front seat of the van was suddenly enveloped in a hurricane of flying bullets.

Khalid Ghani died instantly, not knowing he had been betrayed.

43

On the roof of the restaurant, Sacrette was scanning the town through binoculars. In the distance he could see the lights of the diving, darting helicopters hovering over the nuclear power plant. The chatter of machine gun fire was faint, but distinct.

Donaldson and the others were also on the roof, as was Suleiman.

Sacrette looked at the old Kurd. "It worked. Now, let's hope your telephone call to the police will put the Iraqis on the trail of the others." He looked at Donaldson. "If you've left out one single item, Donaldson, I will personally cut off your balls."

Donaldson shook his head. "I gave you everything—the locations of the men along the pipeline, the group in Baghdad. All of them."

"One question: what was the mission of the group in the Hercules we shot down?"

Donaldson grinned. "Baghdad. After the para drop they were to infiltrate into the city. At midnight, they were going to stroll around town, creating a bit of havoc on the local population."

"You mean kill civilians?"

Donaldson flashed a ruthless smile. "It's a gesture Hussein would have appreciated. After all, he *is* a bloodthirsty bastard."

Sacrette started to say something, but was silenced by the sound of an approaching aircraft.

"Get down," he ordered.

On the roof, the men had their weapons at the ready. Peering over the low wall surrounding the roof, Sacrette could barely make out the outline of the aircraft.

"It's running without lights," Sacrette said. "Get ready."

As the aircraft drifted over the roof, Sacrette waited for the gunfire he was certain would erupt any moment. Looking up, he could see the undercarriage. The markings were clearly Iraqi, but there was something unique—and totally unexpected.

The aircraft wasn't a helo.

It was an Osprey.

The huge turbo props were rotated to the vertical, allowing the aircraft to lower itself onto the roof.

Looking through eyes blurred by the propwash, Sacrette could see the SEAL commander, Brad Davies, sitting in the cockpit. He flashed a sharp salute as he hovered two feet off the roof.

"Get aboard," Sacrette shouted. The port doors opened and the men piled into the transport.

When loaded, the Osprey banked sharply, then skimmed low over the city.

"What the hell are you doing here, commander?" Sacrette asked Davies as he slid into the co-pilot's seat.

Davies chuckled. "Disobeying orders, sir."

Sacrette slapped the SEAL on the shoulder. "I don't know what the hell you're talking about, but you are one welcome sight." He thought for a moment. "How did you know our location?"

Davies shrugged. "I was ordered to destroy the stealth and return to the carrier. After sealing the fighter in the cave we were en route out of the country when I started picking up the radio traffic from the Iraqi army. That's when I knew something was happening. I simply homed in on the locator signal from Major McGee."

"Good thinking, Brad. Thanks."

"You can make my explanations to the admiral."

Sacrette knew what he meant. Davies had put his career on the line, but there were other things to consider. "What is the Iraqi army doing about the mercenaries?"

"There's a shitstorm coming down in a dozen different parts of the country. What did you do, captain?"

Sacrette laughed. "We called the police. They must have sent the troops to stop the mercenaries."

"They've been stopped. Baghdad. Shatt al Arab. Kirkut. All over the country."

"Excellent. Now . . . turn this bird north. We're getting out of this place before the whole Iraqi army comes down our throats."

"What about the civilian?"

"Suleiman?" Sacrette turned and looked at the old

man. He was sitting next to Donaldson, gripping a rope tied around the mercenary's neck.

Suleiman was tired, stained with blood, but undaunted. The CAG reached over and gripped the Kurd by the shoulder. "We're taking him home!"

44

SULEIMAN WATCHED THE YOUNG MAN NAMED BOLlinger attach a detonator to a block of explosives mounted in the opened bay of the stealth fighter. McGee was watching, looking somewhat sad. When ready, Bollinger led the group out of the cave and into the darkness. The stars were brilliant; the wind barely moved.

"Let her rip," Sacrette said to the young demo expert.

A resounding explosion followed; the earth shuddered and the mountain sealed the opening to the cave.

Walking toward the Osprey, Sacrette had his arm around the old man's shoulder. There had not been much time for greetings, as now there wasn't much time for farewells.

"Once again, old friend, you've come to my aid. How can I thank you?"

Suleiman shrugged. "An old man needs nothing but a warm bed and dreams of heaven."

Sacrette extended his hand.

Suleiman's leathery grip was firm. "Good-bye."

The Osprey lifted off, carrying the men from the plateau overlooking his valley. Walking to the rim, Suleiman looked down into the ancient valley where he could hear the flow of the Tigris in the distance.

He knelt, facing the east, where the sun was starting to rise.

He prayed for his village. He prayed for his country. He prayed for the good men of the world.

Then he closed his eyes and fell asleep, perched on the ledge overlooking the valley barely touched by time.

45

SHEIK SHEHAB NERVOUSLY TWIRLED HIS PRAYER BEADS as Ali Akhbar Murjan closed his briefcase and started for the door. There was nothing in Murjan's face to suggest defeat or remorse. A cold, ruthless destroyer of humanity, he moved from one project to the next without conscience.

"We were betrayed," Shehab said simply.

"Yes, my brother. The white devil's betrayed our plan. Such is the fate of the Arab when dealing with the westerners."

"What will I do? I can't stay in Abu Dhabi. The police will come for me."

"You can come with me," Murjan said flatly.

"You old fool. That's worse than death. To live in your country? What would I do?"

"You would be alive."

Shehab laughed. "Alive. I would rather die in Abu

Dhabi than be alive in Iran."

"As you wish," said Murjan as he paused at the door. He shrugged his shoulders, then turned the knob.

Less than three feet from the door, standing in the hallway, Murjan heard the explosion from a pistol.

He paused for a moment, then continued walking to the elevator.

Once inside he pushed the button for the first floor.

The plan had failed.

He knew, without doubt, there would be others. He knew that terrorism was not on a timetable.

PART THREE: OPERATION DESERT STAR

46

0400.

THE LOW WHINE OF THE OSPREY'S ENGINES WAS THE only disturbance on the flight deck, where a skeleton recovery crew was guiding the VTOL aircraft to a landing. When the engines shut down, the doors opened and the personnel debarked to a small welcoming committee. At the head of the committee was Admiral Lord, looking tired, relieved, and concealing his agonizing sense of betrayal.

"Good morning, captain. Well done." Lord shook Sacrette's hand, and staring past Diamonds, to whom he nodded appreciatively, he saw the air force pilot. "Welcome aboard, major."

McGee shook hands with Lord as LeDuc was removing Donaldson from the Osprey. The Brit was still smug looking and walked with an arrogant swagger.

Lord simply stared at the merc with an icy indifference. "Is that the man?"

Sacrette nodded. "I had to make a deal with him, admiral."

Lord said softly, "What kind of deal?"

"Immunity, in exchange for all the information he has regarding the intervention of foreign interests. He told us the mission, but he's holding out on the parties involved. I suspect he'll want to strike a bargain with the boys from State before he says anything else."

Lord called sternly to LeDuc. "Put him in the brig!"

"Aye, aye, skipper." LeDuc replied, pushing the mercenary toward three burly marine SPs.

"You look like you could use a drink," Lord said to Sacrette.

"We all could use a drink."

Lord swept his hand toward the island. "Follow me. I'll be the bartender."

Three decks below, the men sauntered into a mess hall where a small bar had been set up, along with a variety of dishes served up by the cooks.

Sacrette gave Lord a detailed report of the mission from the time they departed Al Salamiyah airbase. When finished, Lord asked about Fallon.

"He figures his mission has been compromised. Therefore, he's contacting the remaining teams and pulling them out. They'll exfiltrate the way they came over—across the Turkish border."

"All things considered, that would be a prudent decision."

"What the hell happened, admiral?"

Lord shrugged. "Once the high command was informed of the private interests, and fearing a major clusterfuck once you went after McGee, it became a game of 'cover our ass.' The decision was made to bring in the diplomatic corps and use a back channel to inform the Iraqis."

Sacrette grumped. "We were expendable." There was no emotion in his voice, just a simple statement of fact.

Lord was fumbling with a paper cup filled with bourbon. "I resigned my commission, captain."

Sacrette rose off the chair. "You what? Elrod, have you lost your goddamned mind?"

It was the first time Lord could ever recall Sacrette addressing him by his first name. He didn't seem to mind.

"Perhaps it's time, captain."

"Time for what? To quit? This isn't the time to quit. This is the time to get ready for a fucking war. These boys are going to need you, admiral. I'm the one that was on the end of that sharp stick. Me and these men, and we're not ready to quit. Not while the threat exists."

Lord gave the words some thought. "I appreciate what you're saying. Christ, I couldn't believe our government would do that. Not to our own people."

"I guess they see the larger picture, admiral."

Lord became somewhat withdrawn.

"It's not too late. You can pull the papers back. You know the chairman. Hell, he's probably thrown your resignation into the trash can."

Lord shrugged. "We'll see."

"In the meantime, what's the situation? Do the SEALs go to Kuwait City?"

Lord shook his head. "The insertion of any covert troops into Kuwait City has been cancelled. It's too risky after what has transpired."

"I figured as much. Damn. That means Mohammad Mostafavi and the royal family are trapped." The pain in Sacrette's voice was genuine.

"Not necessarily," Lord replied.

For the first time in hours Sacrette felt the fatigue begin to fall away. "It's a go?"

"It's a go. If you still want the assignment. After what's happened—no one would blame you for backing out."

Sacrette downed the remnants of bourbon and flashed a grin. "Give us a few hours sleep and we'll be ready. Order a briefing for 1000 in the VFA-101 ready room."

Lord nodded. "It'll be done."

Sacrette started walking away; turning, he spoke while he walked.

"And call the chairman of the JCs. Tell him you had a case of temporary insanity. Tell him you were wrong. Hell, tell him anything. But get back on board. Otherwise, they might promote me to take your place, and we both know what that would mean."

As Sacrette walked away laughing, Lord considered the thought. "Dear God," he mumbled. "That would be disastrous!"

47

0900.

JAZIRA SABAH WAS COMING OUT OF THE PRIVATE QUARters where the royal family was lodged. The guard stood, but she motioned for him to relax. A worried look was on her face as she found Mostafavi sitting with the captain of the palace guard.

He noticed immediately something was wrong. "Is there a problem, your highness?"

"My mother. She has a high temperature. I'm afraid she's becoming ill."

Mostafavi released a long sigh. "What can I do?"

"We need a doctor," she replied, knowing she may as well be asking for the return of her country.

"A doctor?" Mostafavi thought for a moment. "I know a doctor. Whether he'll come or not, I don't know. It would be very dangerous. Not just for us, but for him."

"Why?" asked the captain. "It is for the royal family. He must come."

Mohammad shrugged. "The doctor is an American."

48

1000.

"TEN-HUT!" THE MARINE STANDING AT THE REAR door of the *Valiant* ready room barked loudly as the admiral entered. The men stood sharply, all eyes on the admiral as he strode to the podium. When he motioned, the men seated themselves in their brown leather chairs.

Seated in the ready room were a few pilots, the Red Cell team, and Diamonds, all in the front row. They looked tired, but eager.

"Gentlemen," Lord began, "Captain Sacrette will conduct the briefing." The admiral stepped down as Sacrette took the podium.

"Before we were sent to recover the stealth, we had a mission directed toward Kuwait. That mission is now being resumed. However, there are some changes. The men from SEAL Team Two will not deploy as planned. The current situation creates too much risk. Therefore, it will be a small, covert operation, utilizing myself, CPO

Farnsworth, and the Red Cell team. Details have been worked out to include a change in our operational platform. Instead of crossing the border from a land-based air strip, we'll be using a carrier."

"The *Valiant?*' asked LeDuc.

Sacrette shook his head. "The *Valiant* is too far away. We'll be operating from the U.S.S. *Enterprise,* which moved into the Persian Gulf yesterday and is now stationed off the coast of the United Arab Emirates. We'll launch the mission from the *Enterprise* with a few minor changes."

There was a twinkle in Sacrette's eyes, alerting Diamonds, who groaned.

"'Minor' changes?" Diamonds said to himself. In the past, whenever the CAG suggested minor changes, it generally meant something major.

"Four fighters from the *Valiant's* Red Wolf pack will accompany our element to the *Enterprise.* The aircraft on the *Enterprise* are under their own priority. The four Hornets will be led by Commander Wagner. Rounding out the pack will be Michaels, Thomas, and Stevens."

"What is our mission?" asked Commander Wagner.

"The mission of Red Wolf will be to create a diversion both during entry and withdrawal from the sensitive airspace. As you know, the Iraqis don't have an airborne radar capability. They only have ground-based radar, which is barely adequate. Most of the radar was destroyed during the war with Iran, and last year during Operation War Chariot. They haven't recovered, which should make penetration less difficult. The Osprey will come in low, beneath the existing radar. Once inside Kuwait, we will make contact with a friendly element in the desert. From that location, CPO Farnsworth will accompany a contact into the city and touch base with the prince. When all is set on that end we'll fly in and bring them out. It means moving fast, staying low, and being ready for any unexpected problems."

"What time does the mission jump off from the *Enterprise?*" asked Commander Wagner.

"Nineteen hundred. The Osprey will deploy at that time. The Hornets will wait for my signal to launch."

"What kind of diversion are you planning to keep the Iraqis looking the other way?" asked Lt. Michaels.

Sacrette explained the diversion.

Lt. Thomas laughed. "Sounds like a scenario from *Top Gun* school."

49

1215.

MOSTAFAVI WALKED ALONG THE STREETS OF THE city, which were nearly empty of pedestrian traffic except for the presence of the Iraqi army checkpoints. Most of the troops were deployed around the outskirts of the city, but their presence was felt and known. The air would quake occasionally with the thunder from MiG fighters flying low over the city, as though the noise was a constant reminder to the Kuwaitis that they were the defeated.

Nearing what was now called Saddam Hussein Hospital, Mostafavi walked past the army guards patrolling the front entrance.

Following the invasion, the hospital was closed by the Iraqis with many of the patients literally dumped into the street. Most of the medical equipment, supplies, and even technicians, were packed onto trucks and shipped to Baghdad. The inhumane act provoked the outrage of the United Nations, and the rest of the Arab world, resulting in the eventual re-opening of the facility. Services were now minimal at best. Only those with an emergency could be seen by the physicians allowed to remain on duty.

Approaching a reception desk, Mostafavi clutched his chest and forced a painful look on his face.

"I need to see a doctor," Mostafavi said weakly.

The receptionist began filling out a form. Standing behind the woman was a soldier who watched her every move and listened to her every word. When the form was completed she directed him to the rear of the hospital, where the emergency room was the only section of the hospital receiving patients.

In the ER, Mostafavi sat on a bare table. There were no sheets. Dozens of people were in the room. A young man with a bullet wound in his leg lay on a table. Standing around the young man were several Iraqi soldiers, all of whom seemed to delight in his pain.

Fifteen minutes later, a tall, blond woman approached. Dr. Dorothy Patterson came to Kuwait with her husband, an engineer with the state-run oil industry. She was one of the civilians who refused to be evacuated from the city; wanting to stay for professional reasons, she also had personal reasons for staying. Her husband had been taken hostage by the Iraqis and was now one of Hussein's official "guests." She looked tired. Her white smock was bloodstained and dirty.

Dr. Patterson recognized Mostafavi, whose shop she had visited on many occasions. Taking a chart, she began asking him questions while a soldier stood nearby.

"Are you having pain?"

He rubbed his chest. "Chest pains."

"I'd better listen to your heart. Please pull up your shirt."

She took a stethoscope and began listening to his heart. Leaning close, he was able to whisper in her ear.

"There is someone who needs a doctor."

"Who?" she whispered back.

"A royal patient. An old woman."

Dr. Patterson's eyes joined momentarily with Mostafavi's. There was fear in her eyes. She leaned around behind him and listened at his back. "The soldier doesn't speak English. Tell me quickly. What is her illness?"

Mostafavi explained the situation in a hurried, whispered voice. When finished, he added, "She is where you once bought a gold ring for your husband."

A look of surprise registered on Dr. Patterson's face. Mostafavi nodded reassuringly.

Dr. Patterson put down the stethoscope, then spoke cryptically. "Your heart has an irregular beat, but under the circumstances I can't do much for you. I will give you some pills. Take one pill now, and one at eight o'clock this evening. Do you understand?"

He nodded. *Eight o'clock this evening.*

She went to a cabinet and took two pills from the only remaining pill bottle left in the cabinet. She slipped the two pills—which he noted were aspirin—into an envelope.

Handing the envelope to Mostafavi, she repeated the instructions. "Take one now—and at eight o'clock. Come back and see me tomorrow if the pain continues."

Mostafavi thanked her and was quickly ushered out the rear of the hospital.

Thirty minutes later, he had returned to his shop. Slipping inside he opened the steel door and disappeared into the walk-in safe.

50

1230.

THE OSPREY LIFTED OFF THE FLIGHT DECK AND FLEW west, then south, crossing into Saudi Arabia through Israeli airspace. Thirty minutes later, the F-18s of the Red Wolf pack were locked into the shuttle and ready for the catapult launch.

When the voice of the air boss boomed, "Launch the Alert Five," the four Hornet pilots were ready for the slingshot ride along the catapult.

Minutes later, Commander Laura "Jugs" Wagner was bringing her F/A-18 up to maximum military power. Unlike the heavier Tomcat, the Hornet could launch short of afterburner thrust unless in bomb or strike mode.

Today, she was flying in the fighter mode.

The blast deflector shield rose behind the two firetails streaming off the Hornets' GE-404 engines. Forward of Jugs' cockpit, the launch officer knelt on the deck, checking the flaps, ailerons, and launch bar. When certain all was ready, he pointed two fingers down the catapult tracks.

In the bubble, the cat operator watched as the pressure reached the right setting on the massive pistons operating the catapult, and when satisfied, pressed the fire button.

Steam streaked from the track as the Hornet lurched forward. In the cockpit, Jugs was slammed into her seat by the transverse g's working on her body.

Less than two seconds later the *Strike/Fighter* was screaming off the deck.

Passing the end of the bow, Jugs pushed the throttles through military power into Zone Five afterburner and raised the nose to begin climbing at pure vertical.

At 1545, Jugs and the three fighters were passing over Dhahran, on the east coast of Saudi Arabia. In the distance the water of the Persian Gulf came into view. Off her port wing lay Iraq and Kuwait. Off her nose lay Iran.

The U.S.S. *Enterprise* was stationed to the south, off the coast of Qatar.

Jugs switched her communications system to the *Enterprise* frequency. "U.S.S. *Enterprise*, this is Red Wolf leader. Cruising at Angels eighteen. Requesting permission to come aboard, sir. Over."

"Permission granted, Red Wolf. Have been expecting you. The rest of your contingent is inbound. Captain Sacrette is refueling over Saudi Arabia and will land at approximately 1700."

"Roger, *Enterprise*. Coming to the bird farm with three birds under my wing."

Glancing out of the cockpit, she saw the other three F/A-18s flying on her tail, forming a tactical diamond.

Jugs was about to order the younger pilots to tighten the formation when the voice from the *Enterprise* spoke again. The tone had changed.

"Be advised Red Wolf leader, we have a situation in your area. Do you have fuel to respond?"

The four Hornets had refueled over Saudi and were topped off. "I have fuel. What's the problem?"

"Request you fly an intercept to coordinates Juneau-Zulu-six-zero."

Jugs turned on the moving digital display until the moving map of the Persian Gulf was projecting onto her heads-up display, or HUD. Once the area was projecting, she punched in the coordinates on the HUD and felt the computer take control of the aircraft.

"Red Wolf one requesting instructions."

"Defend U.S.S. *Shiloh Church* against incoming aircraft. Suspect incoming aircraft are Iranian," was the order.

Jugs grumped. "Defend, hell. She can defend herself." The *Shiloh Church*, the BG's newest commissioned Aegis class nuclear cruiser, fresh from the Maine shipyard, was a 567-foot fighting platform of stand-off missiles and nuclear threat capability.

The *Shiloh Church* was now stationed off Kharq Island, which lay dead ahead.

Jugs pressed the mike switch on the HOTAS. "Roger, will fly intercept and tactical canopy."

Commander Wagner knew it was doubtful the Iranians were up to more than harassment tactics, since harassment from Iranian fighters had become commonplace after Desert Shield forces of the United States began parking hundreds of fighters in most every airport along the west coast of the Persian Gulf.

But, she thought, she had to be cautious. In the game

where second place finish was no finish at all, she mentally prepared for combat.

"Wolf pack, go to a two-by-two spread at Angels fifteen, Four thousand foot step-up. Red Wolf two on my three at fifteen. Red Wolf three and four, fly TAC. Keep your eyes open, children, and remember to obey the ROE. Rules of engagement are as follows: do not fire unless fired upon, or certain of eminent attack. Do you copy?"

Flying off her right wing, Rhino Michaels reported. "Roger, Jugs. On your three at Angels fifteen."

Following standard operating procedures, the two remaining pilots checked in with the CAG.

"Roger. Proceeding to TAC," replied Red Wolf three, Gooze Thomas.

"Roger. Proceeding to TAC," replied Red Wolf four, Lt. j.g. Brent "Gompers" Stevens.

Jugs eased the needlenose Hornet onto a heading that would intercept the *Shiloh Church* within minutes.

To the east, Commander Wagner could see the two Iranian air bases; one, at Bandar Khomenyi, on the northeast coast and Bushehr, beyond Kharq Island on the west coast.

The coastline was rugged; brown except where the water of the gulf was a deep blue. Behind the coast, running a jagged course to the north, lay the Zagros Mountains, perhaps the most desolate mountain range in the Middle East.

Leaning to glance forward, she saw the wake signature of the *Shiloh Church* turning a long, white trail in the gulf. Steaming back to the center of the gulf, the *Shiloh Church* was the northern watchdog of the gulf blockade preventing Iraqi freighters from departing with Kuwaiti oil, a blockade against foreign ships bringing supplies to Iraq in violation of the U.N. embargo.

Before Jugs could contact the cruiser, she heard the captain of the *Shiloh Church* give a hurried explanation of the situation.

"Red Wolf leader, be advised, there are four—repeat—four intruders harassing my ship."

Jugs turned on the radar and brought the televised images of the aircraft onto the screen of her horizontal indicator.

A quick glance was all she needed to send a shudder racing along her spine.

"Red Wolf Two, follow me, Rhino. The bogies are not Iranian—repeat—the bogies are not Iranian. They are Iraqi Mirages—repeat—Iraqi Mirages."

"All right!" Rhino shouted. "Let's get it on!"

"Hold your horses, Rhino. Be aware of rules, but be cautious. Consider as potential hostile intruder. Arm your weapons—guns and sidewinders."

In the CIC aboard the *Enterprise,* the warning of the threat made Admiral Kupper reach instinctively for the red telephone linking the carrier with the Joint Chiefs at the Pentagon. Seconds later, the admiral's conversation was being scrambled to the Pentagon, then unscrambled as the Chief of Naval Operations learned of the situation.

"Do not fire unless fired upon. Intent is not to be interpreted—repeat—fire only if fired upon."

Kupper said nothing; he was angry. To give the enemy the first shot violated one of the most sacred maxims of aerial warfare: *Get off the first shot!* That put the aircraft on the defensive, generally burying the fighter's nose during evasive tactics, denying the pilot the use of his own radar weapons systems to counterattack.

Kupper transmitted the CNO's orders.

"Damn!" said Jugs. "They're Iraqi fighters, flying out of their national airspace. Not to mention they're displaying aggressive action against a ship in international waters."

"You have your orders, commander," Kupper's stern voice came back.

Jugs understood, but she wouldn't be caught off-guard. Although she switched off the rocket system, she kept one weapons mode available, the mode most preferred by the fighter pilot: guns!

51

THE FIRST PAIR OF MIRAGES CAME DIRECTLY AT JUGS and Rhino in wing formation, stepped down an identical four thousand feet from the two fighters topside. The two topside fighters were lining up on Thomas and Stevens.

The first pass was close enough for Jugs to see the sun visor on the opposing fighter's helmet.

She bat-turned inside, a manuever the Hornet does better than any other fighter. In seconds, she was on the Mirage's tail.

Playing the buttons on the HOTAS like a piccolo, Jugs switched to her AIM-9L Sidewinders and began sensing the heat signature with the AN/APG-65 radar. When the targetting box on the HUD turned into a circle, she knew she had the Iraqi pilot locked up from heat signature.

She also knew something else: the Iraqi would be

hearing a chirping in his ear, telling him he was locked-up.

That was when the Iraqi did something Jugs wasn't expecting. The Mirage pilot rolled inverted, hauled back on the stick, and executed a split-S.

"All right, you sweet son-of-a-bitch. Break right." She expected the Iraqi to turn tight to the inside and try to get on her tail.

That's when the unexpected happened. The Iraqi went nose up, hauled back on the stick to inverted, then snap rolled an Immelman.

The two fighters were flying straight toward each other, a tactic taught American fighter pilots. A tactic Jugs knew had been taught to *Iranian* pilots by American flight instructors.

That's when she realized the deception.

"They're Iranians—not Iraqis," Jugs was nearly shouting as she streaked past the nose of the Mirage.

Which made sense, since the Iraqis were operating too far from their southernmost base at the captured airbase in Kuwait City.

"Iranians?" came back Rhino, who had his hands full with his own particular dogfight.

"Correct," replied Jugs. "That's why they jumped on the *Shiloh* from out of nowhere. They took off from Iran. The Ayatollah's grandchildren are playing games."

"What next, Jugs?" asked Michaels.

Commander Wagner thought for a moment. "Red Wolf pack, form on me. Break off contact and form on my position."

Within seconds the four Hornets were flying wingtip to wingtip.

"Go to full dirty," ordered Jugs.

The three younger pilots didn't understand, but they followed orders.

Simultaneously, the Hornet pilots lowered their landing gear and flaps.

The Mirages passed overhead in a thunderclap at mach one, then broke off and rolled around behind the Hornets.

"You gotta be crazy, Jugs. We're sitting ducks!" shouted Rhino.

"Trust me, Rhino. They aren't going to fire. They want us to fire. Let's give them a heartbreaker. Fly at MCA."

One of the unique features of the F/A-18 Hornet is its ability to slow its ground speed to almost a trot without stalling. Noses up, power levers forward, the Hornets looked like four roman candles burning over the Persian Gulf.

"They're taking the bait, Jugs," Michaels was watching the Mirages approach from the rear.

The four Mirages were slipping onto the topside of the Hornets, nestling into the slot provided by the Hornet pilots. The Iranian pilots were flying at minimum controllable airspeed but unable to slow to the Hornets' groundspeed, which forced their aircraft to gradually drift in front of the Americans.

"Steady, steady," whispered Jugs to the Red Wolf pack.

As the four Mirages drifted over the top in the game of nerves, Jugs looked up. She could see one of the Mirage pilots staring down at her from the cockpit.

"All right. Hand salute."

Each of the American pilots raised his right hand.

In the cockpit of the Mirages, the four Iranians saw

four Americans extending the middle finger of the right hand.

"Now!" shouted Jugs.

On the Mirages' blind side, the Americans cleaned up gear and flaps, went to afterburner thrust, and rode a carpet of fire beneath the Mirages, who were caught off guard.

At the right moment the Americans raised their noses, then shot straight up in front of the slower-flying Mirages.

Jugs could see the undercarriage of a Mirage slide inches past her canopy as she rose in front of it.

Simultaneously, the twin tongues of flame shooting from the rear exhausts of the Hornets exploded against the noses of the Mirages. The effect was that of an acetylene torch.

The canopies of the Mirages ruptured.

52

1715.

In the *Enterprise* ready room, the pilots of a Tomcat squadron had Jugs cornered. They were laughing crazily when Sacrette, Farnsworth, and the Red Cell Four team arrived. The Zulu Station CAG walked proudly to his exec, who sat beaming with pride.

"That was a nice piece of flying, Jugs," Sacrette squeezed his exec's shoulder.

"She can fly with us, Thunderbolt, anyday." The Tomcat exec, a lieutenant commander, shook hands with Sacrette. They had flown together aboard the *Nimitz*.

Female pilots were considered more a novelty than a reality in the navy, at least where combat situations were concerned. Jugs had proven she had a place like the women in the desert of Saudi Arabia were proving they had a place in combat.

The usual small talk followed, then the CAG requested to be alone with his people. When the ready room was empty except for the personnel involved in Operation Desert Star, Sacrette once again went over the operational plan.

When finished, he looked at Jugs. "It shouldn't be difficult to heat up the situation, but remember, don't push it too far. We want a diversion, not a war! Understood?"

She nodded. "Understood, captain."

Sacrette looked around at the faces. "All right," he said, while clapping his hands resoundingly. "Let's get to the job at hand."

With that, the final phase—the most dangerous phase—of Operation Desert Star was put into action.

53

1900.

THE OSPREY LIFTED OFF THE DECK OF THE *ENTERprise* and flew west past Dhahran, then swung north along the coast where Sacrette refueled with a KA-6 Intruder. After "spitting the basket," the refueling nozzle, Sacrette flew east over the gulf to begin his run toward Kuwait. After dropping to within only a few feet of the water, he turned onto a heading that would take him toward the coast of Kuwait.

"Where in the love of Jesus are we, Thunderbolt?" asked Farnsworth. He was wearing a pair of night goggles. The coast appeared a greenish-white through the STARLIGHT lenses. Below, the waves were close enough to touch.

"Approximately ten minutes from our deployment station, chief," replied Sacrette. His eyes were locked onto the horizon.

"What's our heading?" LeDuc asked Sacrette.

Sacrette checked. "Two-eight-zero."

LeDuc was playing the role of navigator, reading the navigational chart in his lap. "When you cross the coast, turn to three-one-zero. Fly outboard for two minutes. Then turn to two-nine-zero. Fly outbound for eight minutes. You'll see the rendezvous."

Farnsworth said nothing; he assumed the CAG knew what he was doing. Eighteen minutes later he wasn't sure. Through his goggles he saw a small oasis. Dispersed along the edge of what appeared to be drooping palms, he could see the outlines of structures. They seemed to be swaying slightly, as were the fronds of the palms. That's when he realized what he was looking at.

"Tents. There are tents beside an oasis."

Sacrette looked through the windscreen. "That's our rendezvous point. Time to sit this bird down."

On the edge of the oasis, Zayid Maklouf watched the Osprey approach through binoculars. Zayid, a banker in Kuwait before the invasion, was young, in his twenties, with frail features. His hair was short, his eyes dark, Arabic. He was dressed in the traditional robe of the bedouin with a red and white kaffiyeh covering his head. Beneath his arm, hidden in the folds of the flowing robe, was an AK-47.

Moments later, Sacrette rotated the engines of the Osprey, turning the fans from horizontal thrust to vertical, literally turning the transport airplane into a transport helo.

Lazily, the Osprey floated from the black sky in a swirl of sand. After the helo landed, the fourteen men of the Maklouf tribe emerged from their tents brandishing weapons. Most of the weapons were FN FALS. What made the weapons most interesting to Sacrette as he stepped from the Osprey was that every rifle was aimed at his chest.

Zayid approached, speaking in Arabic. Sacrette shook his head, indicating he didn't understand the language.

"You are the friend of a man in Kuwait City?" asked Zayid, now speaking in perfect English.

Sacrette appeared relieved that the language barrier had dissolved. "I have something that belongs to Mr. Mostafavi." He reached into his pocket and removed the flight wings.

Zayid studied the flight wings, then lowered his rifle. "Welcome to Kuwait." He embraced Sacrette for a long moment.

Sacrette thought he felt the young man shiver and was genuinely touched by the sincerity. He was a man who had lost his country; therefore, his identity.

To an Arab, such loss is worse than losing manhood, worse than losing life.

Farnsworth joined Sacrette as Zayid led the SEALs to a tent. Inside, halogen lights burned brightly, fed by a generator purring at the rear of the tent. The tent was roomy, cordoned off to offer private sleeping quarters for the women. In the center, seated on large pillows, Abu Maklouf, the father of Zayid, sat watching the Americans as they approached.

Abu Maklouf appeared to be short and sturdy, though his body was hidden beneath a robe. His powerful-looking neck and strong hands were those of a man used to hardship, unlike the son, who was soft-looking by comparison.

The remarkable resemblance was in their eyes. A deep intensity burned, giving Sacrette an uneasy feeling. He couldn't help but feel grateful these men were on his side and not the enemy's.

"Be seated," Abu motioned to a pillow near where he sat.

They sat, and were served tea. Sacrette loved the sweet, Arab tea. Arabs pour the tea several times from glass to glass before serving, thus breaking down the bitterness.

After a light snack of camel-meat kabobs, Abu Maklouf belched resoundingly. Sacrette did the same. Good manners were important to the bedouin.

Abu rolled forward on his pillow. "My friend Mostafavi said you are a man to be trusted."

Sacrette nodded. "I would not have come had it not been at his request." He held up the wings. "This tells me that you can be trusted."

"Then you believe you know of the location of the royal members?"

Sacrette pocketed the wings. "I believe so."

Abu's face grew serious. "You must keep this information to yourself. Say nothing around my men."

"Is there a security problem?" Sacrette asked uncomfortably.

"We have picked up several 'stragglers.' We don't know who they are, except that they are Arab. There are many stragglers in the desert, trying to escape to Saudi Arabia."

Sacrette understood. There was still a question he needed answered. "How is it your caravan is allowed to roam freely? I would have thought the Iraqis would force you to stay in one place."

Abu shrugged. "Simple." He produced what looked like a passport.

Sacrette opened the document. He nearly choked at what he found. "Jesus!"

"What is it, Thunderbolt?" asked LeDuc.

Sacrette held the travel document. "It's an Iraqi travel document. It says Abu Maklouf is an Iraqi citizen."

The tension began to mount as Abu produced yet another passport. "We are also citizens of Kuwait. We are bedouins. The desert is our country. Borders do not exist. In this area there are political borders, but they are merely invisible images in the sand to the bedouin. We travel freely throughout, from Lebanon to Dhahran, from Iran to Egypt."

Sacrette understood. "Why have you chosen to help the royal family?"

"They are Arab. Descendants of Mohammad. My brothers in Iraq have invaded the land of my brothers in Kuwait. Arab destroying Arab. That is not the way of the Koran. The man in Baghdad must be stopped before the sand is soaked with more Arab blood, blood spilled by Arabs, like Iran, where a million brothers were killed. And for what? Nothing." He spit in the sand. "Now there is talk of chemical gas, of missiles aimed by Arabs toward Arabs. This must stop."

Farnsworth was taking it all in. "Like the civil war in the United States. Brother against brother."

"Yes," said Abu. "Like your civil war. And now, like the slavery that existed in your country, there is an evil shadow spreading across our land. The shadow must be destroyed."

"I like the way you talk, Abu Maklouf," Sacrette said. "I know you are a man to be trusted."

Abu nodded, then cautioned, "Trust no other once you leave this oasis. In Kuwait City, you will see many terrible things. Death. Destruction. Personal possessions are being shipped to the north. The women are being raped. The young men are now being forced to join the Iraqi army. They will be put in the front line if your army invades—without weapons. More human shields. It must not happen."

LeDuc had listened quietly. Sensing there was more, he finally asked, "Why are you running this great risk, Abu Maklouf?"

Maklouf smiled. "Four hundred years ago the bloodline of my family was joined with the bloodline of the Sabah."

Sacrette gulped. "Then the emir is a relative."

Abu Maklouf rose, then faced the rescuers. "The emir is my cousin."

A heavy silence followed. Finally, Sacrette checked his watch. "It's time to saddle up." He looked at Farnsworth. "Chief, you'll have to go in alone. Find Mohammad. You know the place." Sacrette looked at Abu, then asked, "Can you get him into the city?"

Abu clapped his hands. Four women suddenly began pulling off Farnsworth's boots and jacket. They produced a robe and a kaffiyeh. Within minutes, the CPO had been transformed into a passable-looking Arab.

Abu Maklouf spoke. "Zayid will take you to the city. He knows the safest route."

"How do we get there?" asked Farnsworth. "Land Rover?"

Abu Maklouf smiled softly. He led the men outside into the warm desert night. He pointed toward the oasis. The transportation stood waiting.

Farnsworth's heart fell to his stomach. "Jesus. This can't be happening!"

Standing by the oasis, saddled and ready for travel, were two of the ugliest camels Farnsworth had ever seen in his life.

54

2000.

Dr. Dorothy Patterson was kneeling by the bed where the prince's mother lay resting. She had taken her pulse, blood pressure, and temperature three times to make certain there was no mistake. Each examination revealed the same result: the old woman needed to be hospitalized.

"All of her vital signs are poor, Your Highness. She needs to be in a hospital. It's her heart." She was talking to the prince, who was sitting on the edge of his mother's bed. Mostafavi stood near the door with Jazira.

The young prince shook his head. "What hospital? The hospital named for Saddam Hussein? The Iraqis would let her die."

"You're probably right." She looked at Mostafavi. "You said earlier the American government was coming to help you escape. That may be her only chance for survival. Do you have any idea when they'll arrive?"

Mostafavi shook his head. He was beginning to feel like a man with no hope, which forced him to a decision. "If the Americans haven't arrived by midnight, we'll take measures into our own hands."

The prince stood and squeezed Mostafavi's arm. "It may be the only hope we have. Can you make the arrangements?"

Mostafavi thought for a moment. "I can try."

He left not knowing if he could make good his word, but then, he knew he had not been able to make good his word in several months—since the Iraqis invaded.

On the upper level, he slipped out of the shop and moved along the street, staying in the shadows. There was one thought he had, one that would require boldness, and the cold heart of a viper.

Reaching the corner, he knelt in the darkness. That's when his heart fell.

Across the street, a tank was positioned beneath a grove of trees overlooking the boulevard.

The Soviet TU-72 had a crew of four. The four men were lying in hammocks strung from the tank to a tree; one was between two trees. The sound of music coming from the American Armed Forces Radio network played, drifting to where Mostafavi sat watching the Iraqis.

His shop was nearly in the center of the capital, which meant running a gauntlet of Iraqi checkpoints in order to reach the edge of the city. Once there, they could strike straight across the desert.

That was when he realized the futility. There were six members of the palace guard; four members of the royal family. The tank would only hold four, six at best, which would make the space cramped in the event of a battle.

He felt defeated.

That was when he heard the pulsating thump and beat of rotor slap. Looking up, he saw a Huey drift overhead. The chopper slowed when approaching a tall building adjacent to his shop. Watching, he saw the Huey 1-B, formerly of the Kuwaiti air force, flare, then settle onto the roof.

The Iraqis had been moving their helicopters nightly, thus accomplishing several objectives: deploying the heloes as a rapid deployment and deterrent force against the resistance, which was striking mostly at night, and to prevent the choppers from becoming targets on the ground, while at he same time confusing the American reconaissance satellites mapping the military posture of the Iraqi army.

Mostafavi smiled.

Tonight, the helicopter arrived as though guided by Providence.

55

2230.

THE DESERT APPEARED ENDLESS AGAINST THE STAR-filled Arab night. The stars were brighter than Diamonds had ever imagined. The darkness was thicker than any he had known, yet they could see to travel. It was astonishing. And painful.

The ten-mile trek across the desert had exhausted Farnsworth beyond imagination. Riding on the hulking camel, each stride of the animal's long legs was the prelude to another painful jolt for Diamonds. The CPO would rise upward, then slam violently into the saddle, which wasn't really a saddle. It was more a frame mounted on the animal's hump.

"How much farther?" Diamonds hissed at Zayid.

"Two miles. There is a highway. When we reach the highway, we will find other transportation. This was the safest way to cross the desert. Iraqi patrols stay out of the desert at night."

Farnsworth pulled the robe tighter around his neck. "I can see why. It's cold."

"Yes," said Zayid. "The desert is hot by day, cold by night. It is the night that makes the day bearable. Otherwise, the bedouin would live in misery."

Farnsworth's eyes widened. "This is misery, Zayid. Hot, cold, sand, Christ! Why don't you stay in the city?"

Zayid smiled mysteriously. "My roots are bedouin. To the Arab, the desert is part of our heritage. Wherever there are Arabs, there is a desert. An Arab will not live far from a desert, the way the Portugese won't live far from an ocean, our heritage."

Farnsworth thought about that for a moment. "I think I understand. Like being a farmer, being close to the land. Once you've lived there you can't be happy anywhere else."

"You would make a good Arab. You understand what nourishes the soul."

Farnsworth smiled, then grimaced as he was thrown again into the saddle. "One thing's for damn sure. If I lived here I'd trade in this roller-coaster ride for a Cadillac. A Cadillac doesn't drink much water. The seats are softer, and they damn sure don't smell."

Zayid laughed. "Perhaps you wouldn't make a good Arab. Arabs worship their camels."

"I've been shit on, pissed on, and farted on by camels for two days. I have the right to hate the ornery buggers."

Again Zayid laughed.

Thirty minutes later, the talk had trailed off, as had the pace. Slowing his camel to a walk, Zayid paused near the rise of a tall dune. He dropped the reins to the camel and slithered up the dune. Moments later he whispered for Farnsworth to join him.

Pointing toward the highway, Zayid said, "There is an Iraqi checkpoint."

Taking a pair of STARLIGHT goggles, Farnsworth scanned the road. The brilliance of the stars, which is the keystone of STARLIGHT principles, lit up the field of vision as though it were daylight.

"A two-man checkpoint," said Farnsworth. He handed the binoculars to Zayid.

On the highway, two Iraqi soldiers were sitting in a jeep. The jeep still retained the markings of the Kuwait army.

"I count two," repeated Farnsworth.

Zayid rolled over on his back. He stared for a moment at the stars, then rolled back over and again scanned the soldiers.

Wetting his finger, he tested the wind. A slight breeze was blowing from the east, the direction they faced.

"Have you a pistol? One with the device that stops the gun from making noise?" he asked Farnsworth.

"A silencer?"

"Yes. A silencer."

Reaching beneath the robe, Farnsworth produced a Browning automatic pistol. The 9mm auto had a silencer threaded to the muzzle.

"Like my Visa card—I never leave home without it." He handed the pistol to Zayid.

Zayid took the pistol, then quickly explained his plan.

"You've got more balls than a stud fieldmouse, son. I'll say that for you. But question is: can you do this? Can you kill like this? Cold. Brutal. You don't look old enough to have that kind of hard bark."

"I have seen my country invaded. My land stolen. My people raped and murdered. Could you kill if you were a young Kuwaiti with a gun?"

Farnsworth squeezed his shoulder admiringly. "You have to get close. The silencer cuts down on the pistol's accuracy. I couldn't get close. I don't speak the language. You'll have to talk your way to them. Real close, like I said. Then—BOOM!—BOOM!"

Zayid stood. He went to the base of the dune and took the two camels by the reins. Slowly, he pulled the reins and led the camels toward the checkpoint.

After Zayid had gone thirty meters, Farnsworth took an Uzi from his pack, which he wore beneath the robe. Slowly, he stalked down the dune, following in the tracks of the young Arab.

Nearing the checkpoint, he heard Zayid call to the Iraqis. There was the metallic ring of the soldiers loading their weapons.

Farnsworth leveled the Uzi at the jeep, which now had its front lights on.

A voice in Arabic snapped an order. Zayid raised his hands and walked into the flood of lights washing the highway.

More loud orders. Then, laughter.

Farnsworth felt a sickening feeling.

The kid's in trouble!

Farnsworth quickened his pace, then he was thrown to a sudden stop.

The muted sound of the silenced pistol was familiar, and relieving.

Reaching the dark side of the jeep, the two camels stood on the side of the road. Zayid stood in the center. At his feet lay the bodies of two Iraqi soldiers.

A deep, dark stream of blood soaked the road beneath their heads.

Farnsworth examined the bodies. A clean hole through the right eye of each man.

"Good shooting, son."

"*Shukran*," replied Zayid, which meant "thank you."

56

THE LIGHTS OF KUWAIT CITY CAME INTO VIEW AT THE edge of the Iraqi-occupied capital of the tiny nation state, what few lights were burning. The city sat in near darkness. An eerie sight, thought Farnsworth, who was unsettled by the obvious.

"There's no sound, man."

Zayid could be heard taking in, then releasing, a long sigh. "The city has always been so beautiful, especially at night. The lights on the boulevards would dance, like the shimmer of candles off water. Now there is blackness. Where music once could be heard, there is nothing but the shout of silence."

Farnsworth turned sideways and studied the young man. "Christ." He muttered.

Farnsworth was beginning to understand what a man feels when he has lost his country.

Dressed in the uniform of one of the soldiers, Farnsworth was riding the shotgun seat. Zayid was driving the jeep. Diamonds pointed, "Let's take this circus on the road, son."

Zayid laughed slightly. "We must be crazy."

What Farnsworth didn't know was Zayid's knowledge of the city. The young bedouin turned into an alley, then onto a street. Another alley. Another street.

The trip was a journey into horror. Everywhere he looked. Farnsworth saw buildings burned out or darkened. Most of all, there was the silence.

"Don't you have dogs in Kuwait?" Farnsworth asked incredulously. He had not heard the single bark of a dog. Dogs barking was as common to the night world as the moon on a cloudless night.

Zayid shook his head. "The dogs of Kuwait are all dead. They have become a source of food supply. More importantly, they were killed by the people so the Iraqis could not be warned if the resistance was moving about."

Farnsworth shook his head in admiration. "You seem to have covered all the bases."

"Not quite. But we are learning this filthy business."

That was when the eerie silence was shattered by the scream of a young woman.

Jerking to a stop, the jeep was in an alley, nearing a street. Two silhouettes could be seen in the thin light.

Farnsworth stepped from the jeep, followed by Zayid.

At the end of the alley the whimpers and throaty moans of two people could be heard.

When they reached the soldier tearing the clothes off a young Kuwaiti woman, Farnsworth didn't say a word. His powerful fist drove forward, crashing against the jaw of the soldier, who looked dumbfounded, holding nothing in his hand but his dick.

The blow drove the soldier against the wall of a building. He slithered down, then collapsed in a heap.

Taking out his knife, Farnsworth looked at the young woman. She pulled back in fear, seeing a man wearing an Iraqi uniform holding a knife.

"Tell her it's all right. Tell her we aren't going to hurt her."

Zayid explained in Arabic.

The lovely, long-haired Arab woman took Farnsworth's hand. She kissed his knuckles, then disappeared around the corner.

"What do we do with this character?"

Zayid looked at the fallen Iraqi soldier. "He must not be found."

Farnsworth didn't understand.

When the young bedouin stripped off the soldier's clothes and threw the garments in the rear of the jeep, Farnsworth wasn't certain of what was going on.

When he saw the young Arab's knife flash, heard the throat of the Iraqi open, and the rush of wind from the severed windpipe, he didn't need to ask questions.

"Dead bodies are a common sight in Kuwait City. The Iraqis kill for the pleasure of killing. This must look like a Kuwaiti was killed."

Zayid took his Arab robe and kafiyyeh from the jeep and dressed the Iraqi.

When finished, he spit on the dead soldier. "The soldiers will think he's a Kuwaiti."

"Does it work?" asked Farnsworth.

"Yes," Zayid nodded sadly. "The Iraqis never check for identification. They just throw the bodies in trucks that patrol the streets after dawn. What they don't know is that many of the bodies are Iraqi."

"How does that pass muster? How can they not know their men are missing?"

Zayid shrugged. "Many Iraqis have deserted. They desert everyday. We find them wandering in the desert, trying to reach Saudi Arabia."

Farnsworth knew there was a high rate of desertion in the Iraqi army. "Let's get moving. We've got to see a man about a prince."

Following Farnsworth's directions, that is, the name of a street, and the general location, Zayid was able to guide the jeep within a block of the building housing the shop of Mohammad Reza Mostafavi. Parked in an alley, the young bedouin shut off the engine.

They could have gone further, except for the tank sitting at the corner in the park.

"What now?" Farnsworth asked.

"We travel by foot." Zayid got out and asked Farnsworth, "Where is the prince?"

Farnsworth went to the mouth of the alley. He stuck his head out far enough to study the terrain. There was the park. The tall buildings.

"We're close." He pointed. "This way."

Zayid followed the CPO along the sidewalk, hugging the shadows tightly.

Reaching a burned-out part of the building, Farnsworth looked inside. The layout was familiar. A single glass showcase, absent of glass, sat in the rear near a wall.

"We're home."

Squatting, Farnsworth duckwalked to the rear of the shop. Remembering the walk-in safe, he found the panel that would slide open with an electronic prompt.

That was the problem. Farnsworth didn't have an electronic prompt.

Reaching to his neck, Farnsworth removed his dog tags.

He leaned into the wall and began tapping the panel in Morse code.

A dash. *T.*

Four dots. *H.*

Two dots. One dash. *U.*

One dash. One dot. *N.*

One dash. Two dots. *D.*

One dot. *E.*

One dot. One dash. One dot. *R.*

One dash. Three dashes. *B.*

Three dashes. *O.*

Dot. Dash. Dot. Dot. *L.*

Dash. *T.*

Thunderbolt!

Diamonds repeated the process several times. Nothing.

"Perhaps they are gone," said Zayid.

Diamonds shook his head in defeat. "Goddamnit!" He hissed. "They were supposed to sit tight."

"They may have been captured."

Before Diamonds could respond, there was the sound of an electrical whir.

Diamonds looked at the wall and said, "Open Sesame!"

The wall opened.

Standing in the thin light framing his body, a voice Farnsworth recognized said, "Welcome, my friends."

57

On the roof, Mostafavi pointed at the tank sitting in the park. Then his arm extended upward, to the helicopter on the roof of the adjacent building. The presence of one would make the extract difficult and risky.

The presence of both was damned near demoralizing.

"Thunderbolt will be a sitting duck."

Mostafavi agreed. "Before your arrival I had planned to steal the helicopter. If Captain Sacrette tries to pick us up, he could be shot down."

Farnsworth studied the situation. "The tank is easy enough to handle. Do you have a couple of LAWs rockets in your inventory?"

Mostafavi shook his head. "None. What I had was used during the first day of the invasion."

"Damn. What are we going to do?"

Mostafavi thought for a moment. "I have an idea. First, we must get the royal family ready to travel."

Diamonds checked his watch. "It'll take Captain Sacrette about fifteen minutes to get here. That doesn't give us much time."

Mostafavi slipped away to the door leading down from the roof.

Diamonds reached into his coat pocket and removed a small transmitter. Extending the antenna, he turned on the device and pressed a button.

The signal was picked up by the KH-12 reconsat high above the gulf, which flashed a signal to a receiver on the instrument panel of the Osprey.

58

Lieutenant Steve Lipp was sitting in the cockpit of the Osprey. When he heard the sharp report from the receiver, he jumped from the VTOL and hurried into the tent where Sacrette sat with LeDuc and the other SEALs.

"We got the word," said Lipp.

Sacrette sprang to his feet and started for the Osprey. LeDuc and the other SEALs followed. Abu Maklouf was at Sacrette's elbow.

"I will go with you," said the bedouin.

Sacrette looked at him respectfully. "It could get hot once we reach the building."

Maklouf grinned. "I am Arab. I can take the heat."

Sacrette laughed. "You've got yourself a ride, my friend."

Reaching the Osprey, Sacrette fired up the twin engines, rotated the props to vertical and applied power.

In a storm of swirling dust, the transport lifted off like a giant dragonfly.

Once airborne, Sacrette eased the props to horizontal, then eased the yoke forward as he applied full power.

Taking the microphone, he spoke quickly on the frequency monitored aboard the *Enterprise*.

"Red Wolf pack, this is Red Wolf leader. Inbound for extract. Light the candles."

Sacrette shoved the throttles to the wall. The huge transport thundered above the desert as he banked sharp, then leveled off less than twenty feet above the ground.

His eyes weren't on the desert, or the dunes that streaked by. He was watching the faint glow of a few lights in the distance, What few lights that still burned in Kuwait City.

59

2350.

FROM THE COCKPIT OF HER F/A-18 HORNET, COMmander Wagner could see the coast of Kuwait clearly without using the television screen and forward-looking infrared radar. The coast appeared blue through the Cat's Eyes night goggles she was wearing. The cockpit appeared blue as well since the glow from the cathode ray tubes creates a totally bluish environment, unlike the soft green of starlight or red of infrared.

Speaking into the mouthpiece on the crypto frequency, she set in motion the first of many moves necessary to give Sacrette the needed cover to extract the royal family.

"Red Wolf pack, let's go to work."

From eighteen thousand feet, four Hornet *Strike/Fighters* streaked from the sky.

Since the arrival in the gulf of American fighter planes, an almost daily "feeling out" game had existed. Iraqi pilots would swing close to Saudi lines, testing reaction time; American fighters would do the same to the Iraqis, each side determining exactly how much time it would take the other to respond should war come.

The Iraqis responded quickly, more quickly than the Saudis. Only the Americans were the hands-down fastest, what with aircraft constantly in the air or launching from a carrier.

Watching her radar screen, Jugs counted the blips rising off the deck. She knew that in Kuwait City, which lay off the nose, the Iraqis would be looking south, not west.

It was the crack in the floor Sacrette would need.

60

"THEY'RE GOING FOR THE HOOK!" SACRETTE shouted into the microphone. With the Osprey flying low over the city, the CAG was scanning from the terrain rushing by below, to the radar screen where target blips were appearing. "I count four bogies off the deck, moving to intercept."

The radar ident of Red Wolf pack showed the Iraqis closing nose-to-nose as the pack moved closer to the air defense identification zone twelve miles from the Kuwait border.

"Let's hope they keep the Iraqis looking the other way, Thunderbolt," said LeDuc. "We'll need all the breaks we can get."

Sacrette turned to LeDuc. The SEAL was concentrating on the electronic locater receiving the signal from the transmitter.

"Five degrees right," said the SEAL.

Sacrette stepped on the right rudder and banked slightly.

The bean lined up in the center of the locater.

"Dead ahead, Thunderbolt. Keep this baby straight and level. So far, so good."

Glancing out of the cockpit, the city was barely visible. He could make out the military positions along the streets and boulevards. On the roofs of some buildings were anti-aircraft gun emplacements.

Sacrette looked at LeDuc. "I hope Diamonds has everybody ready to travel. We won't have much time. This town is crawling with activity."

61

DR. PATTERSON WAS WALKING ON ONE SIDE OF THE sheikee, as the old woman was called. The captain of the guard steadied her from the other side. The prince was in front, followed by his sister. The soldiers of the guard had taken up defensive positions on the roof.

Diamonds looked at the captain. "Where is Mohammad?"

The captain pointed to the adjacent building. "He has gone to dispose of the helicopter."

Farnsworth was stunned. He hurried to the edge of the building. Looking down he could see the lone figure of Mohammad Mostafavi slip from the shadows and cross the street. Seconds later he was in the alley and gone from sight.

That was when he heard the soft whine in the distance and knew the Osprey was inbound.

"Get them ready," Farnsworth ordered the captain.

62

IN THE ALLEY, MOSTAFAVI HAD REACHED THE WINDing, fire-escape steps extending from the roof of the building. For a moment he thanked Allah the Iraqis had not stolen the stairs and shipped them to Baghdad.

He was carrying an Uzi. Quietly, he started up the stairs.

Minutes later he reached the roof. Moving like a cat, he slid over the edge. The outline of the helicopter was visible in the moonlight.

Inching his way to the chopper, he heard snoring from inside the cabin.

Two men, he told himself.

The starboard door was open. A soldier dressed in a flight suit was sleeping on the rear seat. In the front seat, the pilot was asleep, still wearing his helmet.

Mostafavi's arm rose. The Uzi slammed against the soldier's head. The sickening sound of crushing bone woke up the pilot, who stared wild-eyed at the muzzle of the Uzi.

Mostafavi pulled the trigger. The pilot pitched against the instrument panel, then slumped. Mostafavi grabbed the soldier in the rear and dragged his body out. Climbing into the cockpit he opened the port door and pushed the dead pilot's body out.

Seconds later, the main rotor was churning up the air. When the engine reached lift-off rpm, Mostafavi twisted the throttle and eased back on the cyclic.

The helicopter was rising off the roof when he heard the inbound roar of the Osprey.

THE OSPREY SHOOK THE AIR ABOVE THE BUILDING; the propwash, pushing down from the props, blew the Arabic robes and tore the kaffiyehs from the heads of the men and women charging toward the transport.

Farnsworth was beside Dr. Patterson, who helped the sheikee into the Osprey. Once the old woman was aboard, the doctor took Farnsworth's hand. "Thank you, Mr. Farnsworth. I pray you will be safe."

Diamonds looked at her in astonishment. "What about you? Aren't you going?"

She shook her head. "I'm needed here. I have to stay."

Knowing there wasn't time to argue, Diamonds gave the woman a hearty hug. "You're one helluva lady—lady."

She smiled, then turned and went to the door leading down from the roof. Diamonds stared for a long moment, hoping she would reappear. She didn't. That's when a loud voice jerked him back to reality.

"Get your ass aboard," shouted Sacrette.

Diamonds could see the CAG sitting in the left seat. The Red Cell team had deployed along the roof beside the soldiers of the palace guard.

Diamonds was starting to obey when the building suddenly shook.

The wall overlooking the street was suddenly gone.

Lt. Lipp was visible through the smoke. He had been wounded in his left shoulder. Kneeling beside a dead palace guard, he shouted, "The tank! The tank!"

Sacrette's eyes widened. "Tank? What tank?"

Farnsworth stuck his head through the door. "Get ready to fly. There's a TU-72 down on the street."

"Get them aboard. Jesus. The TU-72 carries ground-to-air missiles. We'll be a clear target."

Farnsworth motioned for the remaining men to get aboard. When the door closed, Sacrette was bringing up the nose. The throttles were at full power and for a second Sacrette feared the airframe would disintegrate.

That's when someone shouted, "We've got traffic! A helo inbound. A Huey."

The CAG felt his stomach tighten. He had nothing to fight with.

Hovering above the roof, Sacrette looked out the window as the helo approached. The cabin lights of the Huey were on. In the magenta glow he recognized the face of the pilot.

Mohammad Reza Mostafavi was hovering directly over the street, positioning his helo between the tank and the Osprey.

A smile was on his face as he raised his hand and saluted. In the next instant, the Huey disappeared.

Sacrette swallowed as he watched the helo dive at a steep angle of attack.

The high-pitched roar of the accelerating helo filled the air as Sacrette began putting the props to the vertical position for departure.

In the next second a tremendous explosion followed as the Huey slammed into the TU-72, which by now was in the street.

A giant fireball spewed up from the street as the tank's magazine ignited; fuel burned red, then orange, then black.

Looking down, Sacrette whispered softly, "Good-bye, my friend."

The Osprey screamed above the city, heading south toward the desert. Near an oil field, Sacrette swung east, staying low until he reached the oasis.

The Osprey stayed only long enough to debark Zayid and his father. The bedouin gripped Sacrette's hand, then kissed the CAG on each cheek.

"May Allah watch over you, my son," he said to Sacrette.

Sacrette nodded his thanks.

Diamonds and Zayid embraced. "So long, kid."

Zayid kissed Farnsworth's cheeks. "I will name a camel in your honor."

Diamonds laughed heartily and climbed back into the Osprey. Ten minutes later the transport crossed the beach and was over the gulf.

Twelve miles from the coast, Sacrette looked through the windscreen to see the Red Wolf pack closing on his wingtips. A sudden sense of relief threaded through his body.

It was over.

Epilogue

THERE WAS NO HEROES WELCOME ON THEIR RETURN to the U.S.S. *Valiant*. It was late in the evening, the sun was setting over the eastern Mediterranean, and the launch crew was conducting recovery operations for the F-14 squadron.

Landing in a Grumman C-2 Greyhound, Sacrette and Farnsworth walked wearily from the transport to the island. They found Admiral Lord on the bridge. He was reading a communiqué that had arrived within the past hour.

Sacrette and Farnsworth saluted. Lord handed the communiqué to Sacrette.

The CAG read the communiqué and smiled when he finished. Handing the letter to Diamonds, he told the chief, "I think the emir meant this for you."

Diamonds read the letter of gratitude from the emir of Kuwait. It was a touching letter; a letter filled with gratitude, words of praise, and the hope that his country might one day be visited again by Diamonds and Sacrette.

Stepping to the coaming, Sacrette looked out over the vast flight deck of the carrier. His hand went to his pocket. Removing a pair of flight wings, he stared fondly at the initials on the back:

M. R. M.

"He was a good man, sir," Diamonds said softly.

Sacrette nodded, then turned and started from the bridge. He paused, turning to the admiral. "What about the Red Wolf aircraft?"

"They're all aboard," Lord replied.

"And the Red Cell team?"

"On their way back to Virginia. By the way, Mr. Feinberg and Major McGee send their regards. Major McGee has returned stateside for a few days."

"What about you? Are you still planning to retire?"

There was a gleam in Lord's eyes. "I'm too young to retire. You were right about the chairman. He said my letter of resignation was misplaced. He never read it."

Sacrette laughed. "Then you're back in the hunt."

Lord nodded. "Back in the hunt."

Sacrette left and went topside to the Buzzard's Perch. The roar of an E-2 Hawkeye screaming off the waist catapult shook the air for a moment as the giant AWAC lifted off the deck en route to its station over Saudi Arabia.

In the distance he could see the coast of Lebanon. His thoughts drifted to the old Kurd, Suleiman Ratab, and his struggle with Iraq. He thought about Abu Maklouf, and Zayid, the brave young bedouin and the others. Fallon. LeDuc. Lipp.

Brave men.

Finally, he thought of Mohammad Mostafavi, and staring at the wings, he felt a strange sensation.

Not of sadness, for that had passed. What he felt was pride. Pride in the men and women he had met in the past few days. Men and women determined to stand up against the evil now looming over the world.

An evil that had to be stopped. An evil that would be stopped.

Saddam Hussein was playing a deadly game in the Gulf. The world was now standing united against the madman. If there was to be war, it would be vicious and brutal. But it would be swift.

Walking to his quarters, Sacrette knew he would be at the front of the battle. Flying his F/A-18 Hornet *Strike/Fighter*, he would lead men into battle.

It was what he did best!

A former paratrooper and combat veteran of Vietnam, Tom Willard holds a commercial pilot's license and has lived in Zimbabwe and the Middle East.